LOOKING FOR TROUBLE

A ROGUE SERIES EXTRA

LARA WARD COSIO

ROGUE PUBLICATIONS

PREFACE

rogue
pronunciation: / rōg/
noun
1. A dishonest or unprincipled man.
1.2 A person whose behavior one disapproves of but
    one who is nonetheless likable or attractive
(*often used as a playful term of reproof*)

1

_____

"Well, Daniel? Are you going to tell me how that makes you feel?"

Daniel. I've told her three hundred times nobody calls me Daniel. I'm Danny Boy. No surname even needed. I'm like my own version of Madonna or Bono. Everyone in the whole of Dublin—hell, maybe even all of Ireland—knows me as Danny Boy. It's all I've ever been called. But *Ms.* Amelia Patterson, my therapist extraordinaire, thinks it's time I go back to formalities. She says it's only right now that I'm closing in on forty years of age and am trying to improve myself. The name, however, like these sessions, doesn't sit right.

I lean down and give Roscoe a pat. He's resting all his weight against my leg in the same way he did ever since he adopted me on the streets of South Korea. He'd conned and charmed his way into my life the way I might have been accused of doing to others before. But as a stray dog in need of a home and companionship, he didn't get too much resistance from me. Now we've been best of mates for going on seven months. We don't go anywhere without each other. He, more than sitting my arse in this overstuffed therapist's chair, has given me the support I need.

But, I have promised my little brother, Shay, I'd keep on with this nonsense. It's sort of an unspoken condition of me continuing to stay at his posh house in the wealthy Dublin suburb of Ballsbridge while he's off in the States with his girlfriend.

The best thing about *Ms.* Patterson, as she insists I call her since as a psychologist she's not technically a doctor, is her penchant for pencil skirts. She's on the thicker side but has lovely legs. Which, along with my reluctance to share my feelings, prolongs my delayed response.

I can't stall any longer, however, so I tell her, "What I feel, actually, *Ms.* Patterson, is a keen desire."

She does her best not to roll her eyes. Apparently, she can see what I'm after. It's not, after all, the first time I deflect this way.

"A keen desire," I continue, "to explore the client-therapist boundaries. I don't see why we can't talk over a drink. Just a wee pint?"

"As a part of your ongoing recovery, you know you shouldn't be drinking alcohol."

"Ah, that's not a no this time, is it? Look at that, Roscoe, she's coming 'round." I give Ms. Patterson a wink and she sighs. Her patience has limits.

Technically, she's right about the whole recovery thing. I've been clean of heroin for just over nine months. Part of the effort to stay that way has been Narcotics Anonymous meetings where they encourage a clean slate from all substances. But I've always done things my own way. I detoxed—more times than I can count—on my own. After twenty-odd years of the back and forth to using and being free of it, being clean has finally stuck. What makes the difference this time? How do I know I won't slip back into that sweet oblivion again? That's what Ms. Patterson wants to know.

Truth be told, she wants to know even more than that. She wants to know my deepest issues, the ones that made me turn repeatedly to the smack. But I don't think she and I know each other well enough for all that—hence the invitation for a drink.

"Let's go back to my original question," she says. She uncrosses her legs and crosses them again, and I fixate on the red mark left on her bare skin. It's from the way her flesh had been pressing together and the resulting mark takes the shape of a heart. A heart that looks stretched out and worn like the neckline of your favorite cotton shirt. "How does your brother moving out of the country make you feel?" she asks.

Ah. Yeah, now that sounds familiar. She had asked that earlier and instead of answering I'd gotten sucked into my own thoughts. Seeing as how she's pushing for a response, I take a deep breath and meet her eyes.

"I *feel*," I say, "fantastic. You know? Like a liberated man, in fact. No one to babysit me or constantly check up on me."

That I've felt almost unbearable loneliness, is not something I'm going to tell her. Not until we've at least had that get-to-know-you drink.

2

B loody typical. I groan and drop my hand, though I don't let my mobile fall. My brother's curt text in reply to my phone call to him has me frustrated.

"Can't speak at the moment. What's up?" he wrote.

You'd think he would realize that it's nearly eleven at night my time. Shouldn't that have warranted a call back? For all he knows, I could be in a jail cell—which has actually happened a time or two and means his texting instead of calling is especially rude.

Stretching my arms overhead, my joints pop and the release is satisfying. I'm in the "Man Cave." It's Shay's glorified game room, really, with a snooker table, dart board, a bar, a sofa and armchair, a large screen television, and a full drum kit. I find myself lounging here into the wee hours more nights than not. There was a time when Shay joined me. Now, I've got Roscoe. I love that dog, but he's a piss-poor games competitor.

I'd grown bored of the MMA fighting I was watching and called Shay to tell him about my session earlier today with Ms. Patterson. I was all ready to give him an earful about the nerve she had in suggesting I've got some sort of issue with being on my own in this big, beautiful house while he's off in San Francisco.

Typing that out in text doesn't sound like much fun, though, so I write back a simple, "Why can't you speak?"

I pat Roscoe's snoring head as I wait for the reply.

"In a car, on the way to a bloody hike of all things."

Shay's response makes me laugh. He's a fit guy, has to be because of his drumming, but he's not really a run-off-into-the-beauty-of-nature kind of athlete. More of a get-in-and-get-out kind of gym guy.

"Don't go, then," I type.

"Got brought along. No choice now."

"Brought with who?"

"Marty. And Ashley."

That bit of information makes me sit up. Ashley must be that "sober coach" who had been hired by my brother's band management to babysit me during the last part of the tour. Though they kept her purpose quiet, I sussed it out pretty quick. Like Shay, I'm good at reading people. But I had no interest in being spied on by yet another person. Turned out she didn't much care to pay me any mind either since she couldn't get enough of our man Marty. *Married* Marty. Not that that seemed to matter to either of them. It was clear as day they could barely contain themselves around each other.

"What are you there for? Try and keep them from going into heat?" I type, imagining the air thick with lust between those two and my poor brother trapped in the middle.

There's a long silence as I wait for Shay's response. I envision him trying to withhold a laugh. I love making that kid laugh.

"Something like that."

Just as I suspected. Marty's about to get some strange. After years of being married to the same woman, he's finally given in to temptation. Doesn't bother me one way or the other. I don't judge other people. Let them make their own mistakes. And let me figure out mine. Each to his own.

"What did you ring me about?" Shay writes. "It's late there."

I knew he'd figure out the time difference eventually.

"You okay?"

Shay's concern is all I need. I suddenly breathe easier knowing that though he's thousands of miles away, he's got my back. I won't bother him with my complaints about Ms. Patterson. He's the one paying for her so-called services, anyway. Going along with those sessions is my ticket to staying in his good graces, which is exactly what I'm determined to do. I've been on a good long streak now, and I'm not after screwing that up. Even if I have begun to feel that itch again. It's the itch to quiet the voices of negativity that have been whispering in my head lately. I call them voices because that's the only way I know how to describe it. But it's not raving lunatic *Beautiful Mind*-style voices. It's more an oppressive certainty that I have no worth and never will.

But I'm not listening. Not this time. No good comes from it when I do.

As if on cue, Roscoe groans as he stretches in his sleep. He's a nothing-special, medium-sized brown dog. But he's got the most soulful eyes and demeanor you'll ever find. Not including Shay, I can't say when I've had a better friend. Roscoe's the one who saved me the last time I got too itchy for a way to vanquish the relentless noise in my head. It's a cacophony of self-doubt and self-hatred, and a conviction that I've got no value. The only cure—or distraction, really—is heroin. The drug served its purpose for years, letting me check out from the world, including the world in me where I found nothing to like. But this has been the longest clean stretch I can remember, and I credit Roscoe for it. Well, Roscoe and Shay. The two each had a big part in getting me to reach for and hold on to basic normalcy.

Being on tour with Rogue, my brother's band, had been the perfect way to keep me focused on something other than finding a fix. I've taken to learning the craft of stage lighting. I think I've got a talent for it, actually, and for the first time in more than a dozen years, I had a real job. Still, the pull to just have a little taste of the H got to me when we were in South Korea. I had to stop that noise in my head, so I set out into the city, sure I'd find what I need. I've done this for so many years, that I can pretty quickly find the right—

meaning *wrong*—neighborhood to get what I'm after. But along the way, I found Roscoe instead.

Or, rather, he found me. He turned out to be the very thing I needed. You might think I poured my restless energy into taking care of him, but really, he took care of me. He asks for very little in return —just for me to be there—and it would kill me to disappoint him. That being said, I'm still beginning to get that ridiculous certainty that if I just try a little smack, this time I'll be able to handle it. The temptation always starts this way, with the argument that I'll only do enough to dull the negativity in my head. It never ends there, of course.

I can't share any of that with Shay. It'd break his heart. He'd probably drop everything and fly here, wanting to try to save me from myself. Then his girlfriend might break up with him. Again. The kid would be miserable. Again. I don't want that.

So, I type a reply to dismiss my brother's concern. "I'm grand, kid. Just had to let Roscoe out for a piss and thought I'd check in with you while I was at it."

"Okay, good."

I can feel the relief in that simple reply. I feel it, too. I don't want to burden Shay with my shit. He's been there and done that. Now is his time to be with his girl and relax.

And me? What is this my time to do? I'm not exactly sure. All I do know is that I'm going to do everything I can to ignore those voices in my head saying I should go back to my old ways.

3

I was five years old when Shay was born. I remember him crying a lot. And I remember loving the sound of him wailing. I loved it because it meant I wasn't alone.

It's that same wailing sound that wakes me from where I dozed off on the sofa in the Man Cave. The lights and television are still on, but I have no idea what time it is.

After a moment, I realize the sound is just an ambulance passing down the street. Not an exact match for Shay's cries, after all. I must have been thinking about my brother in my sleep.

His concern for me earlier with our texts was reassuring. But as much as I take comfort in it, it's also a reminder of how things have changed from when we were kids. I was the one who did the caretaking then. I did that at far too young of an age. With the parents we had, I had no choice.

How my parents ever managed to find each other, let alone procreate, is beyond me. I'd guess it was because literally no one else in the world would have them. They're the most detached and negligent people on earth. When they joined forces, they didn't make each other better as some couples do. No, together they somehow had a complete inability to fulfill the basic duties of parenthood. Oh, and I should mention that though I call them "parents," they are nothing like what that title implies. Sharon and Joe Donnelly did the bare minimum by granting us a roof over our heads and nearly enough food to get by.

I remember treating Shay like he was my living doll. When I saw Sharon prop him up in his crib with a bottle of formula and walk away, I climbed in with him and held him while he drank. I did that even when he was older and able to hold the bottle well enough himself. Ms. Patterson says I got a sense of closeness by taking care of him that I didn't get from my parents, who were only too happy to sit in front of the tele and waste the days and nights away, low-grade drunk the whole time. All I know is that I felt driven to take care of my brother, to be someone he could count on. Because even as a kid, I already knew how it felt to have no one.

I took on the role of caretaker. I wanted to be sure Shay was okay, but I also realized on an intuitive level, that doing so gave me an unfamiliar, but desperately needed, sense of control. Nothing ever mattered to Sharon and Joe. There were no boundaries, no set bedtime, no reminders to brush teeth, or change into clean underwear. There were days when our parents couldn't be arsed to get to the store and we didn't have any food. I'd take it upon myself to chat up the mothers up and down our street, targeting the ones who were open to a harmless flirt from a teenaged me. They brought us in for a good meal now and again. Whenever that happened, I felt victorious, even if it didn't change the fact that we were those kids in the neighborhood who ran wild, the ones the less sympathetic mothers told their own kids to stay away from.

We might have seemed a little feral, but I stepped up and made sure my brother and I were okay. We were inseparable as I did what I could to piece together some kind of normalcy for us, even when that including just getting out of the house and wandering through the neighborhood. I'd pull Shay along in an old wagon when he was only little, and my favorite thing was to try to get a glimpse inside the other houses. To get a view into what real families did. Because I always knew our family was not right.

By the time I was twelve, I'd also taken to minding our parents, making sure they handled the basics like paying the bills and doing the shopping. I forged their signatures on our schoolwork, and made up excuses to our teachers for why our parents could never meet with them. Being the one to take care of everyone was all-consuming. It was just the way it was, but Ms. Patterson has described it succinctly, saying I never had a childhood.

I've never thrown a pity party about it all. I know there are plenty of kids who have it rougher than we did. But I also know it's why when Shay got older and started taking care of himself, I got restless. I was worn down by being the only one to hold it all together. By the time I was sixteen, I was depressed. It was then that those "voices" sunk their hooks into me. It was the vocalization of what my parents had shown me all my life—that I had no value. I internalized those feelings, despite the good relationship I had with Shay, and began to believe that's how everyone saw me.

Then, some friends of mine said heroin gave them a lighter-than-air sensation, like being able to float out of your body. Imagine how that sounded to a kid like me. I didn't resist the temptation very long. And when it gave me exactly what I hoped for—an escape—I never looked back.

I *reveled* in it. It was my fucking due. I made a conscious decision to disappear into addiction just so I could relinquish the responsibility and control that had defined my early life. I've only ever found comfort in chaos since then.

When Shay was only thirteen, I made the mistake of assuming he was damaged in the same way I was. I hassled him a ton, trying to get him to do heroin with me. When he finally agreed, I extolled the ways in which he would feel relief from all that negativity in his head like I did. But he didn't understand what I meant, and it clicked that though we had the same parents and neglectful home environment, he hadn't experienced it the same way I had. I should have let him off the hook and told him I wouldn't stand for him doing drugs with me. But I was too far gone. Too much in that place of selfish need. I wanted him with me on this path because we had always been together.

On the night we were to go to my mate's party to score and shoot up, Gavin McManus came around. The kid was already a legend around school. It was obvious he was going to be some sort of entertainer. He'd come full of his usual bravado and high spirits, oblivious to our intent. His own mission was to take Shay away with him to nick cars for joy riding, which was about as close to the line as my brother ever played. In the end, Gavin won.

Shay choosing Gavin hit me hard. Not because I was jealous, but because it forced me to see the cruelty and selfishness of what I had been trying to do. Going with Gavin was exactly what Shay *should* be doing—well, maybe not the illegal bit, but the part where he was off having a good time with his mates. He shouldn't be throwing his life away with drugs like me. I was disgusted with myself. After spending my whole life taking care of him, of trying to make sure he had a chance at happiness, I nearly pushed him into destroying it all.

After that night, my instinct to take care of Shay reasserted itself. I knew the only way I could protect him like I once had, though, was to leave. Because I also knew I wasn't going to stop doing heroin. It was the only thing that gave me the relief from the voices in my head that I so desperately needed.

So, I went on my way, setting into motion the pattern I'd follow for the next twenty years of getting lost to heroin, finding patches of sobriety, then sinking back into that oblivion again. The longest I was sober was eight months, but even then, I didn't go home to Dublin. Staying away was my self-prescribed penance for having almost turned Shay into an addict. I only went home when I was desperate and needed to lean on Shay for money or needed help detoxing. Then I disappeared again, always knowing that it was better if I wasn't in Shay's life.

But now I've been clean about nine months and have spent a ton of that time with Shay. We don't have that closeness we had when we were kids, but the loyalty we share has never wavered. I've enjoyed being around him and I think he's enjoyed it, too—even if I have made things difficult for him with the odd acting out.

In addition to feeling like I have a brother again, my life includes a dog named Roscoe and a therapist named Ms. Patterson. I've also got an unfamiliar, but welcome, instinct to resist those fucking voices that even in the dead of night pull me back to the reasons why I ever succumbed to them in the first place.

4

My brother has the most ridiculous car. It's a metallic silver 918 Spyder Porsche hybrid with a 900-horsepower engine. It rockets from zero mph to sixty in three seconds. In other words, it's a sports car that'll make your dick hard. If that's the kind of thing that turns you on, that is. Which, given the million-dollar price tag, is exactly what my kid brother is into. With him being in the States, I've commandeered it as my own for the odd trip to the shops, my regular therapy and NA meetings, and most importantly, my mission to find the perfect park for Roscoe.

Dublin, for all its charms, can be an insufferable place when it comes to having your dog off the lead. So many rules about when and where he has to be controlled. The thing is, Roscoe doesn't need a noose around his neck. He and I can communicate what needs to go on without me having to yank him here or there, so I refuse to tie him up like that. That's all well and good except for the fact that I've been chased out of more parks than I'd like by nosy wardens full of an inflated sense of their own importance.

We left the house early this morning to give St. Anne's Park in Raheny on the northside of Dublin a try. Word has it that before eleven, letting your dog off the leash is actually allowed.

As soon as we're out of the Porsche, Roscoe bolts for freedom. Even though this is the second largest park in Dublin proper, I'm not worried. We'll find our way back together.

The sky is mercifully clear, and the sun is gorgeous shining down on the tree-lined paths. Following Roscoe's ever shrinking form, I head left, away from the playground and red brick stables. It's a lovely, long walk during which I spy the Naniken River and a number of late nineteenth century stone towers, most covered in ivy and in disrepair. Roscoe runs back to me several times before continuing to lead the way past Rock Garden and along Chestnut Path toward a small duck pond. I don't see very many other people, just the odd jogger or pair of mothers and their little ones in prams as they power-walk and talk. So far, seems a grand place for my Roscoe, even if I do have to drive us to the other side of town.

I find Roscoe running anxiously from side to side as he tries to sort out how he can get at the dozen or so ducks floating on the pond. Confident in the security of their position, the ducks ignore his agitated yelps and growls.

"They're just for the admiring, Roscoe," I tell him. "No poultry breakfast for you today."

After a time, Roscoe joins me where I sit on a flat rock nearby and we watch the birds together.

"Jesus, no! You eejit!"

It's a woman's voice calling out. The reason for it is obvious in a flash as a yellow Labrador comes racing past us and goes straight into the water after the ducks who have scattered to safety.

"Don't you dare," I tell Roscoe as he moves to join the other dog. I'm not much for rules or convention, but even I know I can't have a wet, dirty dog in my brother's million-dollar car. That'd be a disaster. Thankfully, Roscoe groans but stays put.

The woman who lost her dog to the pond has rightfully given up shouting for him to come back. It wouldn't do any good. The lab is having a wonderful time of it, splashing through the water and muck as if just seeing the ducks inch farther out of reach was his motive to begin with.

The dog's owner is slim with wavy auburn hair cut to just below her jawline. Her jeans, oxblood Doc Martens boots, and paint-splattered, long-sleeve top, suggest she doesn't care much for appearances.

Not that I radiate any effort to make myself all that attractive, I have to admit. My standard is jeans with red and black suspenders and whatever tee shirt smells clean enough. I've got dirty-blond hair in need of a trim, and gray eyes people seem to be drawn to. I know, though, that I clean up pretty well. I've never had a problem getting laid. In fact, I'm damn good in that department—one of the few things I have a talent for, actually. But I've long buried the desire for anything more than a one-night shag. Relationships are impossible to sustain. Either I fuck it up or the woman realizes I'm a mistake. Better not to risk trying to be with someone for more than the quick release.

That hasn't stopped me from thinking about Ms. Patterson, though. *A lot.* I imagine how she might be in bed. How her proper therapist demeanor might be undone by a good fuck. I'd like to ask her *how she feels* about that. Not so much because I fancy her, like, but more to see how it would mess with her. I do love to get a reaction.

"Bum a fag?"

I turn quickly to see the lab owner standing next to me. Hadn't seen her come up. Her useless dog is still in the water.

"Em, yeah, sure." I stand and retrieve my ciggies, giving her one before lighting it. I join her in a smoke and we stare back at the pond. "How long you reckon he'll be out there?" I ask.

"*She* will be there for far too long, I'm sure," the woman replies. "Stupid of me to let her come to this part of the park. I know better."

"This your local?"

The woman keeps her eyes on her dog and nods with a sigh.

I take a drag. "First time for us. Been trying to find a place to go without a lead. Seems a good spot, even if I have to come from Southside."

"Ah, you're one of them poncy Southsiders, are you? Wouldn't have thought it to look at you."

There's amusement in her voice. She's not entirely serious with this dig, yet I'm surprised by the offense I feel. The divide in Dublin between Southsiders and Northsiders is a real thing. And hell, my brother is the prime example of a rich bastard from the Southside. But I'm not like him and—inexplicably— I want her to know that.

"I'm not really a Southsider—more of a world traveler, actually. I'm only there at the moment because I'm house sitting my brother's place. Temporarily. Likely," I stammer on and she eyes me skeptically. Seems her mind's already made up about me and it irritates me far more than it should. But a familiar instinct to make light of this ridiculous divide takes over, and I ask, "How does a Southsider get a day off work?"

Without missing a beat, she glances at me and replies with a saccharine whine, "Daddy, I don't feel well."

We share a laugh at the old joke which makes fun of the stereotype that Southsiders have everything handed to them. The joke lights up her face, makes her seem softer. She's pretty.

I rub my hand clean on my jeans and offer it to her. "This here is Roscoe. And I'm Danny Boy. Good to meet you."

"Danny Boy, is it?" she asked with a smirk before giving me a quick handshake. Like her shirt, her hand has dried spots of paint on it. "I'm Julia O'Flaherty, but I've gone by Jules before since you're partial to nicknames."

Now I laugh. "So, *Jules*, have you been painting house or something?"

"Or something."

I can tell she doesn't want to talk about it, but that's never stopped me before. "Ah, it's more like your job, is it?"

She glares at me and takes her time enjoying the fag she bummed off me.

"Listen," I tell her. "I don't think house painting is anything to look down upon. It's honest work."

"That's very kind of you to say, Mr. Southside."

I groan. Like, out loud. I'm not easily bothered. I've been slagged off by all kinds of people, even ones I care about, without batting an eye. This characterization, though, hits me hard. I hadn't meant for her to take it the way she has. Jesus, why would I? Me, of all people—the heroin addict who has literally no accomplishments to my name.

Instead of trying to get this point across, I lose control over my stupid gob, telling her, "Don't get your knickers in a twist, love. I ain't judging you." The incredulous look on her face makes me realize I'm not doing myself any favors, so I switch tactics. "All I meant is, I've done a bit of everything, too. And a bit of nothing, to tell the truth. Right now, I'm actually in between gigs myself."

"Well, I may be a Northside girl, but at least I'm not unemployed, thanks very much."

"I'm not exactly on the dole. I'm just waiting for things to ramp up again. Then, I'll be—"

"Molly! Here now, Molly!" she calls to her dog.

"Ah, that's her name, yeah?"

Again, all I get is a glare.

Though I'm not sure how our brief meeting turned into this weird debate over Southside versus Northside, I want to leave it behind. It's riled something in me—and her, apparently—that has nothing to do with what we were actually talking about.

"Listen, I've got a towel in the car. I'd be happy to lend it to you and your Molly there. What do you say?"

Jules is wavering, but Molly helps out by running up and shaking her coat in our direction, spraying filthy water at us.

"Yes, I'll take you up on that," Jules says and nods back toward the car park.

Our dogs do the sniffing thing of each other's bits and seem to approve of one another. The four of us walk on through the park, dodging the streams of people who have cropped up in the last hour.

I start several lines of conversation, but Jules isn't interested in any of it. I wonder what I'm even doing offering this woman help. Ms. Patterson might have some insight into my motives, I suppose. It will give us something to talk about other than my shitty childhood.

Jules lets out a peel of laughter as I reach for the door of the Porsche. I turn to see her rolling her eyes.

"Oh, that's perfect," she says. "Typical Southsider."

"It's not my car," I protest.

"Yeah, sure." There's no conviction in her voice as she shakes her head, a smile slowly dying on her lips.

"I'm borrowing it. I don't have one of my own." Retrieving the promised towel, I hand it to her.

"Thanks for this," she says as she uses it to wipe down her dog.

"I'm not joking you. The car is my brother's. He's the wealthy one." I'm not sure why it even matters to me that I convince her of this, but I'm desperate to. "I only even had a job because of him. I was working the lighting for his band's tour up until it ended not long ago. Now I'm just staying in his house and using his car until the band starts back up again."

She had knelt down next to Molly and now she stops the vigorous rubbing of the dog and looks at me. "What band? Who is your brother?"

Normally, I'd shout who my brother is from the rooftops. I drop his name whenever possible, happy to enjoy the perks that come with his fame. But I find myself hesitating just now. I force myself to forge ahead with the answer.

"Shay Donnelly. Drummer for—"

"Rogue."

I nod to confirm. Something passes over her face, some recognition or remembrance. Maybe Rogue was the first band she loved as a girl but hasn't stayed a fan of and now she's flooded with memories. Or maybe Dublin is a small enough city for her to have known the lads back in the day, before they became one of the biggest bands in the world. Whatever it is, she keeps it to herself.

"Anyway, thanks for the towel. I'll have it cleaned and back to you in a few days if you dare come back 'round the Northside, yeah?" she says with a smirk. The playfulness we shared for a second earlier is back. It sends a tingle throughout my body, but she doesn't wait for a real response from me, just turns and pulls her dog by the collar toward a beat up ten-year-old Toyota Corolla.

Watching her go, I'm not sure what to make of what just happened. All I can think is that a drop-in session with Ms. Patterson is in order.

5

There's a sad woman sitting next to a sad plant in the sad waiting room. My therapist's office isn't too far from the Rogue organization's offices in Dublin's Docklands, though it lacks any of their spectacular views of the River Liffey and Samuel Beckett Bridge. Always seemed odd to me the choice of olive green paint for the walls here. So dull. So uninspiring. Maybe Jules can do it up in a nice bright shade of happy yellow.

I'm lost in these thoughts and not even aware of the stink eye the sad woman is giving Roscoe when Ms. Patterson opens her office door. She looks lovely in a gray pencil skirt and burgundy blouse. Her brown hair, usually pulled back when I see her, is now down and in soft curls.

"Daniel!" she says in surprise.

I stand and go to her. "I just need a few minutes. It's an emergency, like."

"An emergency? What sort?"

I start to move past her and into her office, but she puts her hand on my chest to stop me. Her palm is warm. She leaves it there for a second longer than necessary. That feels good.

"Let's make an appointment for another time, shall we?" Ms. Patterson asks. "I have a client now. I can't keep her waiting."

The sad woman takes this as her cue and slips past us and into the office. Damn. Unless I follow her in and sit on her lap, I've lost my chance.

"Well, when can I see you, then?"

"This is my last appointment for the day. First thing tomorrow?"

"No, I've got to be at the park in the morning."

"Well, if it's an emergency maybe you can alter your plans for the park a bit?"

She's let go her professional detachment. In its place is amusement at my expense that I don't appreciate.

"Listen, if you can't do your duty as my therapist to help when I need it, then I'll find another course of action."

"You are not to threaten me, Daniel," she says sternly.

"I'm not threatening you, *Ms.* Patterson. Fuck's sake. I'm asking for your help, amn't I?"

She surveys me for a moment, her mind at work. I pick at my cuticles, a habit I've never been able to curb. Roscoe decides we'll be here for the duration and makes himself comfortable by leaning heavily against my leg.

"Wait until after this session. But I don't have much time. Will that do?" she asks.

"It will. Thanks."

———

Forty-five minutes later, I'm sitting in my usual overstuffed chair in Ms. Patterson's office. I passed the time trying to figure out what I wanted by coming here. But I still can't formulate the words, and Ms. Patterson is not even pretending at patience anymore.

"Daniel, just start by telling me what you were doing before you came here," she says.

That's easy. I tell her the facts of my day: looking for a park for Roscoe; walking through St. Anne's; coming across the woman with the uncontrollable lab.

"And? What more?"

I'd stopped at the part about the lab splashing around in the muck. I laugh as I think about the question. What more do I really have to say? I don't even know. Like so much of what I find myself doing, I don't know what really propels me. I just follow blindly what I think is some sort of imperative action.

"Did you speak to the woman?" she prods.

"Em, yeah. After she bummed a fag from me. We talked a bit. She's some sort of house painter. Was covered in dried up bits of paint. But seemed a bit defensive about the job."

"Okay."

There's a deadly long silence as she waits for me to speak again.

"That was weird," I continue. "But later I lent her a towel from the car. And when she saw Shay's Porsche, I went on about how it wasn't mine. I don't know why, but I needed to make it clear to her that I wasn't the 'poncy Southsider' she'd accused me of being. I don't know her, but I was desperate that she have the right understanding of me."

She lets that hang in the air for a minute.

"We haven't yet talked about your relationships with women," she finally says.

"And we don't need to. What I'm getting at has nothing to do with being attracted to this woman."

"No?"

I fight over a response to this one. Yes, I was drawn to Jules. But that wasn't my overriding reaction to her and I say as much.

"Okay, let's go back a tick. This woman—the house painter—you said she went on about her Northsider status?"

"A bit. Felt like she was teasing me more than anything."

"Flirting?"

"Em, no. It wasn't like that."

"But you wanted it to be?"

I shrug. "Wouldn't have minded."

"You grew up Southside. Your brother's house is still Southside."

"I grew up Southside, but I didn't become one of them, did I? Never had it easy like those spoilt brats."

"True, you didn't have it easy. You made a life of having it rough, didn't you?"

"What's that mean?"

"You've spent the last twenty years chasing heroin, chasing after a rough way."

"And? As if I wanted it like that? Is that what you're saying?"

She tilts her head but says nothing.

"Listen, I don't know what you're after with this, but I'm not a masochist. The H was the only thing that ever saved me."

"Have you ever considered that being an addict is what you thought you deserved? It was the most you could expect for yourself after what your parents filled your head with?"

This strikes way too close to a truth I've taken pains to ignore.

"I was talking about this woman, Jules. You're off track," I tell her.

Sensing I'm not open to her last question, she retreats. "Jules, then. You got twisted up trying to prove to her that you're not some rich Southsider and you don't know why. Is that it?"

Taking a deep breath, I exhale and nod.

"Daniel, this does not constitute an emergency. I really have other pressing business. We need to wrap this up and return to it at next session."

The idea of walking out of here right now sends my heart racing. I can't go without something to help calm the cycle in my head. It's the self-destructive litany of abuse that's slowly begun to get louder since the tour ended and I found myself living in Shay's big empty house. It's the abuse that crept up a notch after my encounter with Jules. I came here for a reason, and I'm not leaving until I get some kind of relief.

"It's pressing business to *me*," I tell her. "Jesus, help me out here. Just tell me what you think's behind it so I don't obsess anymore. 'Cause when I get those obsessive thoughts in my head, the only release I know is smack. I've already been teetering on the edge and I need *help*. Take pity if nothing else."

This confession hangs heavy in the air. I feel the heat of her gaze on me as I look away.

"First," she says carefully, taking a moment to uncross her legs and press her thighs together as she smooths her skirt, "I'd recommend you attend an NA meeting as soon as possible. And agree to a sponsor already. There has to be someone you can connect with."

"Yeah, yeah." I get up and Roscoe rouses himself, too.

Ms. Patterson stands as well. "Second," she continues, "my initial impression is that you're scared you've lost your identity."

"What the—"

"That this woman sees you as a posh Southsider is terrifying to you because it's true. You're not the addict anymore. You're not the one running away from things anymore. You've learned a trade and have the promise of a job with your brother's band. You are responsible for—at the very least—the wellbeing of your dog. These are all good things. But they're also so foreign to you that you're willing to use the discomfort of it as an excuse to ruin it all."

Again, she's veered too close to something I don't want to think about. Her assessment means that I've, for once in my life, broken away from that old version of me, the one intent on destroying everything. But yet, that's the only me I know. If I admit that's not me anymore, then who the fuck am I?

"Or," I say, a wicked grin coming to my stupid gob, "maybe it's just that I've had it with being strung out all this time and I know how to handle myself when it comes to H, so why in bleeding hell shouldn't I give it another go?"

She's absolutely still for a long moment. I'm not even sure she's breathing. Or if I am. I said it to get a reaction from her, of course. That's what I do. I say things without much thought other than to see what'll happen. But now I'm worried that I've sent her into some sort of therapist freak out. I know I'm a handful, but isn't she trained for this shite?

"Daniel," she finally says, "I want to get your permission for me to speak with your brother."

That is nothing like what I thought she'd say.

"Em, what the fuck for?"

"I'd like to speak with him about other ways to support you since he's no longer in Dublin."

"Nah, you won't be hassling my little brother with this. You're stuck with me, Ms. Patterson. Do your job."

Clearly, this doesn't please her. Her shoulders drop, and she eyes the floor. The weight of her disappointment is palpable. Normally, I couldn't care less to appease someone else. I don't let others' expectations of me change a damn thing. So, I don't know what it is that makes me think twice now. She's doing her best, I know that much. I've fought her every step of the way and she's kept coming at me, trying to find new ways to connect. I've come to enjoy my time with her, even if I spend it dodging her efforts to break through to something meaningful.

"I'll call him myself. To check in and have a chat. How about that?" I ask.

"It's a step in the right direction, I suppose."

"What more? Honestly, what more can I even do?" I'm asking with sincerity. I did come here looking for answers from her—even if I'm not above vetoing the ones I don't like.

"What about Gavin McManus?"

I laugh at the non sequitur. "What about him?"

"Listen, Daniel, you're an unconventional client—we both know that. So, I'm trying to provide some equally unconventional ideas for you. If you won't let me bring your brother into this and you won't get a sponsor at NA, would you be able to speak with Gavin about some of your . . . temptations?"

"Why him?"

She sighs and throws up her hands. "He had his own run at drugs, didn't he? That's what the tabloids all detailed. And what he's even admitted to."

I scoff. Gavin McManus' cocaine binge a few years back is the stuff of public record, yes, but it certainly doesn't mean we have some sort of unspoken bond. I get on with him well enough, but we've never been about sharing our afflictions. For the life of me, I can't imagine going to him about this. He'd surely tell Shay, for one.

And he'd also tell his fucking boyfriend Conor Quinn, too. I don't need Mr. Perfect lording anything more over me than he already does. Quinn tolerates me, but only for Shay's sake. No, I need to get her off this idea.

"Being an addict doesn't mean you instantly understand every other one out there. Thanks, but I'll skip on that one. Now, how about that wee pint?"

A smile comes to her lips before she can stop it, and she shakes her head ruefully. "I'll see you on Thursday."

"Aye, you will." I pause. "What's the difference between a Southside man and a Northside girl?"

Wariness returns to her gaze and she waits me out rather than ask the proverbial "what?"

"Northside girls have higher sperm counts."

The joke only elicits a headshake. It's a stupid play on the stereotype of Northside women being tough and Southside men being soft, and we both know it. Still, I couldn't resist. I never can.

I summon Roscoe and we're off. The visit offered no resolutions, but I've come away feeling better. Rather than analyze why exactly, I just latch on to it and hope it lasts.

6

It doesn't. It doesn't even last long enough for me to get to the car park before I start obsessing over whether Ms. Patterson is blowing me off or if she really has other business to get to. She seemed rather eager to push off her responsibilities onto Shay or Gavin, didn't she? Like, she couldn't wait to be done with me. But was that because she really thought I needed that other support? Or because she can't be bothered to deal with me if it doesn't fit neatly into our prearranged fifty-minute sessions? Not knowing the answer gets me riled up again as I start toward the car and then head back toward Ms. Patterson's office building. I repeat this pattern of indecision several times before I decide my next move.

Why go home without any answers when Roscoe and I can wait outside her office to see what's what? Sure enough, fifteen minutes after my session, she steps outside, and we follow her as she walks several blocks before waving wildly at a group of three women in front of the Bord Gáis Energy Theatre. Bloody hell. Her "pressing business" is meeting her girlfriends to see the musical *Spamalot*.

Roscoe and I watch the ladies gab for a minute before they head next door to The Marker Hotel's Brassiere restaurant. The space is made up of glass walls and high ceilings and it's easy to see them seated at a table with brown and yellow leather club chairs in the main part of the restaurant. They are swiftly presented with a bottle of red wine, which they use to make a toast. Lovely. I can almost hear Ms. Patterson tell them over wine and a laugh why she was late to meet them. Surely, she'll say it was one of her crazy clients who unexpectedly delayed her.

I have no internal debate, just start walking. Ignoring the gasp and protests from the girl at the hostess stand, I head straight through to the dining area, Roscoe at my side. The room hushes by degrees as I go until it's utterly silent.

Ms. Patterson is looking at me aghast, wine glass frozen in her hand halfway to her mouth.

"This?" I say to the startled group at the table. "This is your *pressing business?*"

"Daniel, this is outrageous—"

"I'll tell you what's outrageous. You knocking off our session—our very *intense* and *intimate* session—for this nonsense," I say, purposely making our therapy session sound like something sexual. Just to embarrass her. I know she can't or won't rebut this characterization in front of her mates or all the restaurant diners now watching. It would go against the privileges of our client-therapist relationship. I never said I was a saint, right?

Before Ms. Patterson can utter a word, a man approaches me and grabs my arm. "Excuse me, sir, but I need you and your dog to leave immediately." His nose is wrinkled in distaste as he says the word *dog.*

I rip my arm away from the guy and Roscoe leans protectively into me, ready to pounce if I so much as give him a nod of approval.

"Aye, I know this woman, here," I say.

The man looks at the table and Ms. Patterson, her face a mask of disappointment, nods. She takes the white cotton napkin from her lap, folds it, and stands up.

"Let's go outside to talk, Daniel," she says.

As we make the trek toward the front of the restaurant, conversations start up again, softly at first, and then with a few derisive snickers to go with it.

"You all can fuck off back to your boring meals, can't you?" I shout and the silence returns.

"Daniel!" Ms. Patterson presses her hand into my back, pushing me along.

"Ah, lighten up. These sorry sods will only be delighted to take home the story of the fella who intruded upon their lovely dinner, won't they?" I laugh out loud at the shocked look on the turtle-like face of a man waiting by the hostess stand. "I gave their dull lives a bit of excitement for a second, is all."

"This is *unacceptable*," Ms. Patterson tells me as soon as we're outside. "You followed me from my office?"

"Your date with your pals for drinks and a crap musical is the reason you needed to cut me short?" I return.

"That's *not* your business. You must respect the boundaries of our therapist-client relationship or we won't have one at all. Do you understand me?"

She's got the schoolmistress act on, complete with stern face to go with it. But I'm not having it.

"You pushed me out of your office when I was ready to break because you wanted to have a fucking laugh. That's what I understand."

"That's just not true. Think back on what we talked about in that 'emergency' session."

"If you're going to mock me, then, I'll—"

"Stop now. Stop this, Daniel. You've got yourself worked up and it's not based on reality."

"What the fuck does that mean?"

"It means you're not accepting what has really gone on. You're letting your fears take over and color things."

"I saw you plain as day with my own eyes. You couldn't wait to run off, all so you could gab with your friends."

"Listen to me. We spoke in my office. We talked about your visit with the woman in the park and the feelings it brought up. We talked about what was behind it, that you've lost a sense of identity. I suggested speaking with your brother. I suggested an NA meeting. I suggested you speak with Gavin McManus. We agreed to speak more at our next appointment. All that led to us parting in my office. I did not push you out. You *know* that."

This recounting matches my memory. Which means she's right about why I followed her, that it was born out of an error in my perception of things. It's terrifying how well she can read me. She sees my motives well before I do. And now I've got the sinking realization that I've fucked up. It's not the first time. What is different, however, is the accompanying, unfamiliar feeling of regret over it. It's not that I regret crossing her boundaries and ruining her evening. No, I regret that I may have jeopardized whether she will see me again as her client.

Fucking hell. She's the only person I have. Literally, the only person I speak to in person on a regular basis now that my brother is in the States.

"I'm a fucking idiot," I say, mostly to myself. I use my open palm to smack the side of my head repeatedly. Roscoe whimpers and shifts but I don't stop until Ms. Patterson makes me.

She pulls my hand away and slowly lowers it to my side before releasing me.

"You've had a lifetime," she says, her voice calm and soothing, "of poor impulse control. I'm going to take that into consideration right now. I'm going to let this go for the time being, and we'll talk more at our next session. Right, Daniel?"

There's nothing I can say. I'm so relieved that I want to pull her into my arms and give her a huge hug. It takes all my restraint—something I possess very little of—not to. I nod and turn away.

"The play?" she asks. "It's crap, is it?"

She's already let me off easy. This is going even further. I've earned no right to this, but I'll take it in a heartbeat.

Looking back at her, I shrug. "Don't know. Never seen it."

She smiles and shakes her head as if she knew that all along. I'm full of shite, but she's somehow okay with that. Suits me just fine.

"Enjoy, yeah?" I tell her with a smile.

7

The next morning it's lashing down rain, but I still load Roscoe into the Porsche and head out to St. Anne's with the hope that Jules will be there. I can tell by Roscoe's grunting he knows it's a fool's errand, but he's loyal to the core and would go out into the deluge with me if I actually forced us. The lot is empty when we get there, though, letting us off the hook from getting drenched. I pick a spot at random and park anyway.

Fiddling with the car's high-tech equipment, I recline the driver's seat and lean into it, content to listen to the rain tapping against the windshield. Roscoe rests his warm head on my leg and settles in, too. I didn't sleep well last night as I tossed and turned, struggling to bury the whole episode with Ms. Patterson.

I didn't call Shay like I said I would. No reason to bother the kid. He's got his hands full with Marty making a spectacle of himself anyway. Seems the idiot was caught shagging that Ashley in some cabin out there in San Francisco.

I didn't go to an NA meeting, either. Instead, I picked up take-away curry and went home.

Shay was a bachelor for most of his life, but somewhere along the way he bought an ivy-covered brick, two-story, detached house with five bedrooms and a wrought-iron gate outside and had it professionally decorated. The kid did okay. It's masculine without being a bro-haven, and it's put together without sacrificing comfort. It's too big, though, which only intensifies the solitude I feel there.

Last night, Roscoe and I puttered around, then played darts before settling in to watch *Fair City*, purely to mock the melodramatic storylines of the soap opera that's almost as old as I am. But then I got caught up in it and sat glued to the screen like an idiot until the end. I spent the next hour doing a web search on one of the actresses from the show, Sondra Delaney. She wasn't the youngest thing on the screen, but she was blonde, cute, and had a great rack. Imagine my disappointment when I found out she had once been "linked" to Conor Quinn, Mr. Perfect himself. She didn't quite have the same allure after knowing Quinn had been there first. Still, there were enough photos on the web of her in low-cut blouses for me to get the release I needed in order to finally fall asleep.

I dreamt I was in a church, watching a wedding. At first, I thought I was there to witness Shay and his girl Jessica do the deed. But then it became clear that the groom was Conor and the bride was Sondra. Only, they weren't them. They were playing characters like they were the stars of *Fair City*. Halfway through the ceremony, it started to rain. Not outside like you'd think, but inside the church. It didn't bother anyone. We all just kept up the wedding charade as the water came down in steady drops.

There's a sharp tapping at my driver's side window and I start awake. I've dozed off and am disoriented for a few seconds. Was I recalling last night's dream or was I dreaming it all over again? I'm in the Porsche. Roscoe is whimpering, caught up in something outside the car. The rain has let up.

Then the tapping again and I turn, braced to see a park warden or a garda trying to chase me away.

Instead, I see Jules. She's standing outside with the towel I lent her rolled up under her arm.

"Do you want it back or not?" she asks impatiently.

I get out and our dogs reacquaint themselves with the sniffing routine while I stretch out the kinks from my unexpected nap.

"Wasn't sure I'd see you 'round here again," Jules says.

"And why not?" I ask with a sniff. "It's our park now, too." My back's up in anticipation of more hassle over being a Southsider, but she surprises me by going in another direction.

"Well? Care to get out in it, then?"

I eye her for a beat, trying to see if she's fucking with me. The paint splatters on her hands are fainter and fewer. She's wearing a loose gray jumper on top of overalls and has a simple barrette pulling her hair away from her face. Her expression is guileless.

Tossing the towel in the car, I close the door and lock it up.

"Yeah, let's do."

We start off the same way as the day before but at a crucial point, head right instead of left to go in the opposite direction from the duck pond.

"So, do you make a habit of sleeping in car parks?" she asks.

"Not usually, no." I leave it at that. I've never been prone to embarrassment over such things. If I allowed that, I'd never stop the scarlet from coming to my face with all the stupid things I've done.

"That's good. I'd have to reassess our park meetups if so."

"What, are you saying you'll overlook my being a 'poncy Southsider'?" I ask with a laugh.

She stops walking and after half a step, I do too.

"Listen, I may have laid it on a bit thick yesterday. I don't even know why it came out like that. I really don't care where you're from. It makes no difference to me."

"You're sure about that, are you?" I don't believe her for a minute. She and I both had too big of a response for it to have fizzled out this easily. Hell, I made a fool of myself rushing in for an emergency therapy appointment. It had to have come from somewhere real.

"You'd do well for yourself to accept what I'm willing to give you, Danny Boy. For fuck's sake, I don't even know you."

That makes me laugh and I stare at her with a lingering smile. I'm definitely intrigued by her, though in the back of my mind I'm still wary of her reaction when I mentioned Rogue. There's something there that I need to sort out. I may have no qualms about using my baby brother's fame and wealth to my advantage, but I'll be damned if I let anyone else do the same.

"Right you are," I say. "What can I tell you about myself, then?"

"Let's just have a walk. No need to get into it, yeah?"

"Yes, of course."

We continue on and the silence between us is comfortable. Even though I know it would be wise to follow her lead, I can't go for more than a few minutes without speaking. It's a lifelong condition. I get antsy. I pick at my cuticles. My leg bounces when I'm sitting. I'm just not one for letting things lie.

"So, I had a thought. A lead on a painting job if you're keen for one," I tell her. "It's an office, like, so not house painting, but it is in a sad state of affairs. The ugliest, drabbest green you've ever seen. Thought you could spruce it up."

She glances at me skeptically. "This would be your office?"

"No, not mine. My therapist's. It needs a cheerful coat of something."

"Your therapist?"

I can see her stifle a laugh at my expense, but I don't care if she knows I'm seeing Ms. Patterson.

"Yeah. Started up with her for my brother's sake. But I think I actually like her."

"And she's asked you to arrange a paint job for her office?"

"Nah, that's all me. Can't imagine she'd say no to it."

Jules' eyebrows bounce in amusement. "Well, I wish you luck on that, but I'm not a house painter. Or office painter."

"Well, then why in bleeding hell do you have paint all over you?" I blurt out, feeling like she had somehow led me astray.

She stops walking once more and I follow suit. "You really have a limited imagination, don't you?"

"Then you're an artist, is that it?" I should have known. It seems everyone has a hidden talent they simply must explore.

"Something like that."

"Why all the mystery, Jules? Not proud of your work?" I'm teasing but also not. Her evasiveness is getting annoying. What's the point of sharing a walk if she won't share anything about herself? Might as well part ways if that's how it's going to be.

"No, that's not it."

"Well?"

"It's just not something I usually share with men. It's more of a woman thing."

That intrigues me and before I can stop, I say, "A lesbian thing, is it? Didn't peg you for that but doesn't bother me."

She laughs. "You remind me a little of someone, you know?"

"Someone brilliant, charming, and handsome, I suppose?"

"He was, but what I'm reminded more of was his lack of filter. He'd say things without always thinking them through like you seem to."

"Gotta live on the edge somehow, don't I?"

"Is that as wild as you get?"

"Now that I'm done with heroin, it is."

She blinks at that. There's no good way to tell someone you've been a heroin addict, so might as well just throw it out there and let the chips fall where they may.

"You're clean now?"

"Have been for almost a year. Spook you?"

"It'd take a lot more than that, Danny Boy."

"Seen it all, have you?"

"Enough, anyway."

I nod, and we continue walking. The easy banter falls away to silence but has left its mark on me. It feels incredible to get on so well with someone, but I realize she still hasn't shared much.

"Maybe you should tell me a little something more about your-self?" I ask. "So we've both got a bit of exposure, like?"

"Like what?"

"I dunno. Something personal, though. Something on the level of what I just told you."

She contemplates this for a moment before a smile turns the corners of her mouth up. "Okay. How about this: I've fucked Gavin McManus."

8

I can't bloody believe it. She one-upped me.

"Recently?" I ask. The idea that Gavin has ever fucked anyone other than his "great love" Sophie is incomprehensible. The sap has made a career out of songs mooning over her.

"No, not recently," she says with a sigh.

I think she's disappointed I haven't fallen over in shock. Thing is, there's not a lot in this world that would truly shock me. I've seen too much shit during my years of running from one party crowd to another. See, I wasn't your stereotypical junkie living destitute in drug dens. No, I tended to make "friends" with people who had money—trust fund kids, stock market bros, actors, musicians, and the like—who wanted to play a too little close to the line. I was their good time guy who knew the tricks of the trade, like how to heat the H on the spoon and inject it just right. These so-called friends felt safer doing hardcore drugs with me because I made it seem so easy and harmless, and in return I got a free ride. But there was always a time when I knew I'd overstayed my welcome and had to move on.

Of course, it wasn't always the glamorous life. I've experienced the need so deep that I did just about anything to satisfy it, including taking the needle from someone's arm after they've passed out with their high just in case there was enough of the stuff left to at least stave off my itch. I've spent plenty of time in neighborhoods most people can't even fathom. The depth of poverty and hopelessness in those areas is the drug pusher's dream. That's the easiest place to find a fix. It's also an easy place to get roughed up for no reason other than you had the nerve to make passing eye contact. I'm no fighter but being strung out will give you enough urgency to at least put up a defense. I was once losing in a scrape against some fella looking to release his frustrations with the world on me when a prostitute no more than twelve years old stopped to see if either of us was up for a go. The guy beating up on me saw fit to release me and go with her.

You'd think shit like that might make you reevaluate your choices in life, but when you're hooked, there's not a lot of passing judgment —on yourself or others. We were all just getting by, trying to drown the voices in our heads.

Which should give me some sympathy for Gavin given he has had his own struggles, but when I look at him I just don't see someone damaged. He's lived a privileged life for so many years, had Sophie in his corner, and seen unparalleled success with his band. On top of all that, it seems he's also had the pleasure of being intimate with my new friend, Jules.

Then it clicks in my head why she had that reaction yesterday when I told her about Shay being in Rogue. It wasn't some fond memory of having been a fan back in the day, it was the fact that she has history with McManus. It makes me wonder at her motives for being friendly today.

"You still in touch with him, then?" I ask.

"No. We had a . . . falling out years back."

"What kind of drama was that?"

Jules laughs. "The Sophie sort. We were together for a while. Then he went and got engaged to her. Still, we kept our friendship for years after that. Then, he dropped me when he was separated from her. Haven't spoken to him since."

"And now you've come upon me. Am I to be your ticket back into Gavin's world? Is that what this is?"

"Oh fuck off, Danny Boy," she says dismissively. She quickens her pace.

"Just a simple question, love. I'm not presuming anything. Go ahead and set me straight," I tell her as I match her gait. "Go ahead and tell me you came to the park on a rainy day all so you could return a fucking *towel* to me. I'll believe it if that's what you want. I really don't fucking care."

Once more, she stops abruptly and turns to me. "I came here on a rainy fucking day to walk my dog. What were *you* after? Sleeping in your car and waiting for what? For me, yeah? Why? So you could interrogate me about Gavin McManus?"

"I'm not the one who brought him up, for fuck's sake."

"Then *what* do you want from me?"

"I'm not asking anything of you. I don't even—"

Before I can register it, she grabs me by the back of my neck and pulls me to her, pressing her mouth to mine. My confusion at her abrupt change from anger to seduction quickly dissolves as our lips part in unison, tongues desperately exploring each other. I wrap one arm around her slim waist and slide my other hand through her hair. She smells amazing. It's something floral, clean. Her lips are incredibly soft and warm. I'm lost in her.

And she's a ball of need, pushing herself against me and kissing me like I'm the man she's been waiting for all her life. Only, I know I'm not that. She knows I'm not that either. It doesn't matter to either of us, though, because in this odd, random connection, we're each getting something. I don't dare to question it. It feels too fucking good to be touched and wanted by another human who isn't just a mindless drunken hookup. It's been too long since I've had this feeling. I haven't allowed myself to really desire another person in years, convinced that the sentiment couldn't possibly be returned since I'm such a fuckup.

She pulls away to catch her breath.

I don't give her a chance, pulling her back to me, holding her face in my hands as I kiss her like it's the last kiss we'll ever share. For all I know, it will be. This unexpected snog has no chance of lasting.

She'll come to her senses any moment, and she and her dog will run off, never to return to this park just to avoid me. I know it with every fiber of my being, even though she continues to kiss me fiercely. Her hands are on my lower back, pulling me closer to her. She must feel my cock hard against her belly, but still she doesn't stop.

I'm vaguely aware of Roscoe leaning against my leg. For the first time since I found him in the streets, he's not my primary concern.

"My place," Jules says, "it's not far."

That tingle I felt yesterday when she was teasing me about being brave enough to come back to the Northside returns. This time, though, it's got a whole other subtext.

"Let's go," I say.

9

We don't talk as we head toward the car park. Rather, we walk, stop and kiss, and then walk some more. It's not the fastest way to go, but who the fuck cares? We've found some sort of insatiable connection here and it's demanding to be indulged.

When we get to our cars, she tells me to follow her and I nod, silently praying she's not going to ditch me somewhere along the way.

"What do you say, Roscoe?" I ask as we drive. "You think this will keep on or will she back out?"

Roscoe just eyes me and I pat him on the head.

Jules wasn't kidding about living close by. She's a seven-minute drive to an attached red-doored home in Howth. She slides right into street parking but Roscoe and I spend a few minutes searching for a spot with enough room not to endanger the Porsche.

"This is it, buddy," I tell Roscoe as we make for Jules' place.

I'm fucking nervous. Like I haven't been in I don't know how long. At least as far as being with a woman is concerned. I've had the stray one-nighter here and there, but this feels like something different. Not only because I like Jules, but because it feels dangerous. There's more to her motives with me than I fully understand. It may have to do with McManus or it may be something else. What I do know is I'm not going to let any of that stop me.

The red door is open a few inches. I take that as the cue that it is and Roscoe and I enter. The house is small, but the bright white paint job makes it feel open. Roscoe finds Molly straight ahead in an enclosed patio, past the kitchen/dining room combo and adjoining living area. He helps himself to her water bowl. The furniture and decor are minimal. I'm accustomed to more space after staying in Shay's big house. This place is definitely meant for a single person.

I hear music down the hall to the left and follow it. There are two closed doors, but the last one is open and is where the sound is coming from. I can't identify the music. It's something atmospheric rather than melodic. At the door frame, I stop and peer in. The lighting is a soft glow. Two of the walls are covered in mirrors. There is a paint drop cloth covering the entirety of the floor. Photography equipment is staged in a corner. A black padded massage table sits in the center of the room.

Jules has discarded her jumper and is leaning against the table. She's got on the overalls I noted before, but with nothing underneath. A striking tattoo of flowers in vivid greens, blues, and fuchsia forms a sleeve on her left arm. Her right shoulder is covered with a black and white lotus flower. Her skin is otherwise smooth and white, the swell of her breasts exposed through the arm holes of the overalls. She makes that ridiculous garment look good.

"Nice place," I say and take a step toward her.

"It's no Southside mansion, but I like it," she replies with a wink.

I move closer to her and she watches me with a heated gaze. There's no confusion about what's about to happen between us. We both know what this is, and the anticipation is delicious.

"This your workspace?" There's a neat row of small bottles of paint, brushes, and other equipment along one wall. I don't see any canvases or easels, though. Nothing is displayed on the walls that aren't covered with mirrors.

"It is."

I still don't know what her work is, but I lose interest in finding out when she leans her hands on the table behind her and in turn her chest thrusts forward. There isn't much fabric covering that chest and I reach out to unclasp her overalls. Though this move is abrupt and completely lacking in seductive finesse, she doesn't seem to mind. Instead, she catches her breath as my fingers take hold of the metal hooks. She wants this. She wants me. Her desire radiates off of her and I freeze.

Before going on, I want to put her mind at ease over something.

"Listen, I had no choice but to go through a rather intense physical before I went on tour with the lads—for insurances purposes—and everything came back clean," I tell her. "I'm a lucky bastard. Just thought it'd be right to make that clear."

"That is a relief," she says. Then she opens the hand she had closed in a fist to reveal a foil packet. It's a condom. She places it on the massage table behind her, a small smile on her face.

I can't quite read her. It's almost like she's mocking me.

She places her hands over mine, as if wanting to put an end to my confusion, and helps me release the catch on the straps of her overalls. As the straps fall, she lowers my hands to her bare breasts and it feels like I've come upon treasure. It's too much good fortune to have her beautiful tits in my grasp.

"What do you want with a guy like me, Jules?" I ask. Though I'm not going to be the one to stop this, I'm curious how we got here. I pull my hands away only enough to be able to rub my thumbs over her hardened nipples.

Her reply is clear in both action and words. She places her hand over my crotch and says, "I can think of only one thing at the moment."

That's enough to set off another torrent of kisses. Unlike before, when we were at the park, we have nothing to hold us back and we've soon stripped each other of all clothing. She's slim but has a nice shape to her figure. Her small-ish breasts are firm, and she has a minimal patch of hair between her legs. While I've been examining her, she's been returning the favor. I've never given my body much care or thought, but I know I've gotten a lot fitter over the last six months, and she obviously sees enough to like because I can tell she's still that ball of need.

I know what she wants from me and I'm eager to give it to her.

She's just as eager and that mutual desire has us reaching for each other with the same kind of desperation we had when we first connected. There's something that happens when we touch that I can't explain other than it feels like that first spark when a match is dragged over the strike line. Together we *catch fire*.

"Tell me what you're going to do to me," she says.

But I'm not one for talking. I'd rather show her.

I grab a handful of her ass and hold the shaft of my hard cock with the other, guiding the glistening tip to tease her clit. She moans into my mouth as I kiss her, and I feel her nails digging in the skin of my shoulders. Mirroring the quickening of her breathing, I rub her faster until playing like this makes her come with an uncontrollable cry.

As she's recovering, I grab the condom and slip it on. Turning her by the hips, I lean her over the massage table, stretching her arms over her head so that she holds the edge to steady herself against the way I'm about to fuck her. Her face is turned to the side and I follow her gaze to see she's watching us in the full-length mirror on the wall. She likes a show, I realize.

I test that by giving her a firm slap on the ass and see her smile in response. Without pushing myself into her, I lean forward and let the heaviness of my cock rub between her ass cheeks while I kiss and nibble her neck. Her skin is soft and sensitive to my touch. My bites leave red marks. Her whole body will be marked before I'm done.

"Give me your arms," I tell her as I finally push into her.

Obediently, she offers her arms to me and I grab her at the elbows, bringing our hips together with a satisfying smacking of flesh each time I simultaneously thrust into her and pull her to me. In this position, I can see her tits in the mirror. We both can. She's still watching.

I'm close, so I release her elbows and instead wrap an arm around her waist to pull her to me so we're both standing. I lower my face to her shoulder and my other hand finds her clit again. She holds onto my hand with both of hers, guiding me in frantic movements.

And then we both find our orgasms.

10

"Tell me what heroin is like."

We're lying on the massage table. I'm on my back and she's on her side with her leg thrown over mine. We've just fucked each other raw and have barely reclaimed our breath when she comes up with this request.

"No," I tell her.

She trails her fingers over my neck and down my chest. "Why not?"

"Because that's fucked up and I'm not going to do it." Besides, I've heard it before. It's a common come on line, especially by women who are curious about trying it themselves but need a guide. Sort of like what I used to do with my party crowds. But the women who try this angle are much more dangerous because they're usually looking to get deep into it and want to pull you along with them. Now I've got my answer for what she was after in being with a guy like me.

I disentangle myself from her and sit up.

"Don't go," she says, touching my back. "I was just curious. That's all."

Standing, I remove the condom, tie a knot in it, and look for a wastebasket. There's one in the corner and I make use of it before pulling on my clothes.

"I've done loads of coke," she tells me. "With your man Gavin, in fact. I just figure it's a completely different high than heroin."

"Is that what you *figure?*" The disgust is naked in my voice. I'm angry she's turned this amazing sexcapade into something dark. I don't want any part of it. Or at least, I don't want any part in recognizing that what she really wanted was less to do with a connection with me than the connection to heroin I could give her. Just when I thought I could have something real with someone. At least I got a good fuck out of it.

"Hang on," Jules says. She's pulled on her jumper and has grabbed my arm. "Listen, I didn't say it right. I'm not looking to get high or to make you slip. I was asking because I know why Gavin went crazy with coke. I know why he needed that kind of high. His spirit was broken, and he needed something to lift him up. Coke makes you feel like you can conquer the world. But from what I know about heroin, it just slows everything down. I don't know why someone would want that."

The high I got from heroin was definitely the opposite of what cocaine does. H is a depressant, so you get very relaxed. It almost takes you into a trance. But it's the best kind of disassociation because with it comes intense relief. All your worries and demons disappear and are replaced with the singular sensation of happiness. It's a void that you readily fall into time and again, because when the high is gone, all the things that tormented you when you were sober are there waiting and so the cycle of using starts all over again.

I get stuck on the vivid memory of how fucking good the high was and only vaguely notice Jules watching me. Even the ritual of prepping to inject the stuff was satisfying. Just thinking about it stirs that need inside of me and I start calculating where I can find a hit.

11

Jules squeezes my arm, forcing me to blink away the seductive thoughts.

"I was just trying to understand you," she says.

The idea that she wants to know me is lovely. But I'm still stung by my conclusion that she was using me for a drug connection. I'm wary to share any more than I already have, lest it opens the flood-gates of temptation I've been fighting against.

"How about *I* understand something about *you?*" I tell her.

"Okay. Like what?"

"Like, what is this room? I mean, it's a good spot to fuck random strangers, but what else is it?"

She stares at me for a moment before smiling, then laughing. "First, just so we're clear, I don't make a habit of bringing random strangers here. To fuck, that is."

"Do as you like, doesn't matter to me."

With a roll of her eyes, she turns away. "With that attitude you won't be getting a second invitation."

I realize my misstep in appearing too casual. It's just, I don't know what the fuck is going on here to begin with. Should I be presuming some sort of claim on her because we had mind blowing sex? The reason I told Ms. Patterson there was no need to talk about my history with women is because I don't have one. I've never had a real, lasting relationship with a woman. Just fiery, drug-fueled connections that burned out before they could even start. This stuff doesn't come naturally to me, and, in fact, I more often than not say the wrong thing to people in most situations, not just the ones of the intimate sort. I want to tell her not to take it personally, but I recognize just in time that I'd better not open my big gob.

"So, yes, this is where I do my work. It's an art studio. But the art is not put onto canvas or paper. I paint on bodies. Women's bodies."

She turns to face me with this pronouncement, once more expecting to have surprised or shocked me. But I'm neither. So she's artsy-fartsy. That's all well and good.

"It's for a cause," she says. "It's not about being salacious."

"Okay." I shrug, and I can see the frustration build in her face. I suppose that means I'm to show more interest.

This disconnect is what Ms. Patterson and I have been "working" on. It's ingrained in me, she says, from the way I was brought up by my parents. Or not brought up, I suppose would be a better description. All that led to what Ms. Patterson calls the "pattern" of my life of never really being able to get close to anyone else. I scramble to remember the ways she taught me to "consciously" connect.

Clearing my throat, I say, "I'm interested in knowing more." It comes out stilted, like I'm doing my best to speak a foreign language but get the syntax all wrong.

Jules looks at me like I'm from another planet. Might as well be for all she knows. But she's willing to let it go because she goes off telling me about her work.

"Have you ever heard of boudoir photos?" she asks.

"Em, no."

Jules tells me they're all the rage with brides-to-be who want to give their grooms a sexy gift. They'll go to a photography studio, sip champagne to get up the nerve to strip down to lingerie or maybe nothing at all, and do their best provocative poses. The only element

Jules supports of that whole exercise, however, is the idea that it might give women a feeling of empowerment.

"But what about single women?" she says.

I'm lost on the whole subject but figure I'd better go ahead and support whatever she's after. "Yeah, what about *them?*"

"Don't they deserve to have a moment where they can feel good about themselves? Where they can look at their bodies and like what they see?"

"Damn right." Might as well go all in on this.

She nods, encouraged. "I've always painted and started a while back with making my own body the canvas. It was just for fun and experimental, but then I thought, this is the perfect way to reach the women who won't be up for boudoir photos. I can make their bodies into art, something they'd be proud to display a photo of in their homes, because it's not erotic. It's a celebration of the female form."

"Exactly so." I'm on a roll.

"Once I got a few women willing to let me try it with them, I found that it really hit the mark. They were moved to tears by how empowering it felt."

"Ah, that's beautiful, isn't it?"

"It's caught on pretty quick in the last two years or so. It's enough so that along with the royalties from my music, I can make a living."

I'm half checked-out and it takes me a second to get the part about royalties. "What's that? What music?"

This kills her buzz. Her face had been animated and now she deflates. She had been amped up about being a part of empowering women and I've focused on the wrong thing.

"I'm a singer. I've put out three albums. I did a single with Gavin once," she says dismissively. "But I was never anything big. I have no desire to play the tits and arse game required to get any attention in this industry. And anyway, I was never after trying to be the next Katy Perry. I always wanted authenticity in my music. But that doesn't get you anywhere in this celebrity-obsessed world. This art— it's what I want to be doing now. *This* has meaning."

Still a bit thrown by just how much of a relationship she seems to have had with Gavin, I nod slowly. It raises my defenses once more, making me wonder what her motives really are. Gavin McManus is the singer of one of the biggest rock bands in the world. As much as I believe in my brother, Gavin's the reason for Rogue's success. If Jules was once close with him, that meant she had access to all the favors his fame offers. It's intoxicating being in his world. Everything is possible. I can see why Jules would want to re-establish a connection with him.

"Why'd you and Gavin fall out?" I ask.

She hasn't been privy to my thought process just now and is perplexed. Shaking her head, she covers her face in her hands for a long moment. When she looks at me again, her eyes have turned hard.

"I want nothing to do with Gavin fucking McManus, okay? He's in my past. And if you somehow think me hooking up with you was part of an elaborate plan to get with Gavin again, you're seriously delusional. And in any case, I'd like you to leave."

Fuck. I've screwed this up. "Wait a second," I protest, holding up my hands.

"No. Fuck off with yourself." She gestures toward the door.

"Jules, I was only curious. Every time you mention his name, it builds up to something more you had with him. For fuck's sake, I went from not knowing you from Adam, to you saying you fucked the man. Then you did coke with him. Then you were a singer and fucking collaborated with him?"

"So what?"

"So, what'll it be next? Have you a love child hiding away somewhere?"

"Jesus Christ on a bike. Get out, will you?"

"Look, I'm not delusional. I'm just not one for coincidences. I know better, is all. I've played more cons than you can imagine."

She considers me for a moment before speaking. "You're saying, I somehow figured out who you were, waited until you randomly showed up at my local park, chatted you up, and decided fucking *you* would be the way to get back with Gavin McManus, a man I haven't seen or spoken to in years?"

"Well, when you put it that way, it sounds bloody ridiculous," I say with a laugh.

She's not amused as she stands with hands on hips and a scowl on her face.

But she is sexy as hell, with that jumper riding up just enough to torture me over wondering whether she put her knickers back on or not. I need to know what's under that top. Fuck, she's got my cock lurching toward her.

If she can switch gears in a blink of an eye from anger to desire, so can I. I take a step closer to her, lust in my eyes. She puts her hand on my chest.

"Danny Boy," she says firmly.

"Jules," I return with a smile I hope is charming. I let my hands drop to her hips, my fingers toying at edging the sweater up. "You're the sexiest thing I've ever seen, love," I tell her. "Maybe we should focus on the area where we get on. How about another go, yeah? This time, let's take it slow."

She doesn't move away. I can see her chest rise and fall a little more quickly. "Why would I want to do that?" she asks with a weak effort at defiance.

There's no logic to why we've found this chemistry together, but it's undeniable. I lean in and kiss her slowly. She takes my mouth and gives me pressure back.

Pulling away, I press my lips to her neck, whispering, "If I have any talent at all, it's in knowing how to make sure the woman I'm with comes hard. I did that before, didn't I?"

With that last question, I stop teasing and finally reach beneath her jumper. I've found my answer. There's no fabric in my way as I trail my fingers between her legs. It's barely perceptible, but she moves her thighs apart for me. She catches her breath in anticipation of my next move. I watch as she swallows and releases a soft moan. Her skin is silken, warm, ready.

This is her response. I made her come up against the table earlier.

And I'm going to do it again now. Because this is what binds us. No reason to fake an interest in body painting as a method for women's empowerment, or for her to try to *understand* me. This is as real as it needs to get, and underneath it all, we both know that.

12

Avocado green. Not the lovely creamy green on the fleshy inside. The dark, unhappy green of the craggy skin. That's what I've decided the paint color is in Ms. Patterson's office. It's hideous.

I turn my eyes away from the walls to stare at the woman herself. She's been letting long pockets of silence go by, waiting for me to say something. The odd thing is that I've been letting them go by, too. The topic *du jour* is why on earth I followed her after my last impromptu session. Her efforts to get me to explore and talk through my motivation are of no interest to me, however. As with most of my spontaneous misadventures, I don't dwell on thinking over the impetus. I simply move on. Shay has always been a reluctant admirer of my ability to let things go.

Ms. Patterson doesn't seem to share that view. She's tapping her pen against her notepad and pressing her lips together in a terrible attempt to hide her frustration.

"I don't know what else to say," I tell her.

I've already explained that a cycle got wound up in me and that the only logical thing I could think to calm it—other than heroin— was to follow her to see if she had told me the truth about needing to cut our time short. It doesn't occur to me that she's looking for an apology.

At least not until she finally releases a breath and tells me that's what most people would do in this situation. She leaves out the word *normal* to describe "people" but the implication is clear. Most *normal* people would have known better than to follow their therapist away from the office. Most *normal* people wouldn't have then interrupted their therapist while she was having a private get together with her friends. Most *normal* people would have spent some time thinking about what had happened and come ready to both talk it over and apologize.

"I am sorry, okay?" I tell her. "I hope you were able to enjoy your evening after that. I really do."

She seems caught off guard by this. I guess that makes sense since I've done nothing but avoid any acknowledgement of improper behavior since I got here. My mind has been stuck on Jules this whole while.

When I left Jules' house yesterday, it was without any kind understanding of what our time together meant. Well, besides the fantastic sex. That part was clear enough. But despite her protests otherwise, I can't stop thinking about her connection to Gavin McManus and what it means for why we hooked up the way we did.

"Thank you for the apology, Daniel," Ms. Patterson says. "Now, why don't we talk more about your encounter with the woman in the park?"

Even though she's all I can think about, I don't want to talk about Jules. Not with Ms. Patterson. I'm not sure why, but I've lost the burning desire to share with her all the unformed emotions Jules brought up at our first meeting.

"There's nothing to say. We already went over it, didn't we?" I tell her.

"You were very upset when you came storming into my office after meeting her. We should investigate that further."

"You told me your diagnosis, though, didn't you?" I lean down and rub Roscoe about the ears.

"Well, we barely scratched the surface of it. It would be good to talk more about how it impacted your sense of identity—"

"The identity you said I didn't have, yeah?"

"I think you know what I mean. You've shed your old self. It's natural to feel some vulnerability now as you try to understand who you are without it."

I don't want to do this. I don't want to "work" on myself like this. I've got other things on my mind. I need to get her to stop.

"Here's what I understand," I say abruptly. "I saw her again at the park yesterday. She invited me back to her place and I fucked her. Okay? So, what does that tell you?"

Though she doesn't break eye contact, her expression changes. Something hardens as she puts up her defenses. We both know she's not always kept up on that front, though I sense she would end our sessions if I ever acknowledged that. She has either purposely relaxed her professional distance with me or done so without realizing it. Because we've now had two moments where it's become clear that she is uncomfortable with her own actions—first when she flat out diagnosed me as losing my identity rather than getting me to conclude that myself, and now when she's let a tinge of jealousy show. She doesn't like that I was with another woman. That makes these visits a whole lot more interesting.

"What that tells me," she says carefully, "is that you haven't corrected your impulsive behavior over the last couple days after all. And that, in fact, it's escalated."

I roll my eyes. "What is wrong with being impulsive, anyway? I don't see why it's automatically a bad thing. It sure didn't feel bad yesterday, I'll tell you that. And I can assure you that I made sure Jules was completely satisfied."

A blush comes to her cheeks, which I find amusing. Surely, she's heard far more intimate things in her line of work than what I've just shared. Then again, maybe it's that she's actually keen to hear more. Maybe the idea of my tryst with Jules turns her on. A sort of vicarious thing.

With that in mind, I lean forward and lick my lips, slowly biting the bottom one while I watch her.

"It was probably that impulsivity that made it that much hotter," I tell her. "I mean, this was fucking for fucking's sake, you know? You ever . . . indulge in that? Maybe find some bloke in a pub, lock eyes, and then meet in the toilets?"

Ms. Patterson doesn't grant me the satisfaction of a reply. Instead, she turns to a fresh sheet in her notebook and makes a note.

"You should give it a try sometime, if you haven't. That kind of pure sexual gratification is what I got from Jules. That's why once wasn't enough."

She digests this for a moment before asking, "Meaning you'll be seeing her again?"

I laugh. "No. Meaning, I fucked her once. Then once more not long after."

"I see." She clears her throat and jots something down on her notepad once more.

"It was clear from the get go that we were only after a good fuck. This isn't some grand love story. It's unlikely I'll see her again. And that's fine with me. I'd have thought you'd want the same."

She looks up at me quickly. "What does that mean, Daniel?"

"Haven't you said I'm here to sort out my life? I imagine you would say I should stay away from other women and relationships. That I should focus on us."

"Us?"

"Well, we have a thing going here, don't we?"

This suggestion triggers something in her. She slaps her hands down on the notepad hard enough to startle Roscoe.

"Our time is almost up," she says. "But, I think you need another reminder of our boundaries. I have no interest in you other than a professional one. I am your therapist. Not your friend. We are not in some sort of 'relationship.' What we are doing here is trying to explore ways to give you better control over how you manage your decision making. It's about understanding the impulses that led you to your addiction and other poor choices."

She's trying to snuff out the spark between us. That's her duty, I suppose, in her position. Doesn't mean I believe our connection doesn't exist. Not for a second.

13

When Roscoe and I pull up to the house, I see a figure huddled under the archway of the front door trying to stay out of the rain. The visitor's slight size tells me it's a woman, though she's hidden under a hoodie. Shay isn't the type of rock star who gets random groupies showing up at his house. He's a good-looking kid, but he's shy and never courts attention. I'm guessing this is some sort of charity or sales call.

Prepared to give this unwelcome stranger the brush off, I get out of the Porsche with Roscoe at my heels.

"Not interested—"

I stop when Jules turns to face me. *What the fuck?*

She's done one of my maneuvers by showing up somewhere uninvited. It's interesting to have the tables turned. I can see how off-putting it is.

"I never got your number," she says. "Or I would have called."

"About *what* exactly?" I ask, an edge in my voice. Her pursuit of me here, to an address I never gave her, throws my understanding of what we had off kilter. I had left her place thinking we were just hooking up with no expectations. What is she really after?

"I dunno. Just about getting together again."

"I just saw you yesterday. And you're desperate to see me again? *Really?*"

She cringes at my mocking tone and says, "Is it so hard to understand that I fancy you?"

Of course it is. I can't remember the last time a woman pursued me for more than a one-nighter. I've felt all my life like I've repelled, not just women, but everyone. I was brought up being shown I had nothing to offer. Enough years of that and you believe it. Ms. Patterson would say that I've not only believed it but reinforced it by pushing people away or otherwise making myself someone others don't want around.

"How did you find this house, anyway?" I ask, ignoring her question.

She shifts from one foot to another. Her cheeks are red, but it isn't from the cold. She looks small as she hugs her arms across her chest. In a flash, I see in her the same thing I've been dealing with—deep loneliness.

"I figured it out on the internet. It was easy enough with one of those Rogue fan sites."

It always seems to come back to Rogue with her. The wind picks up sharply and rain comes at us sideways. Roscoe paws at the front door.

"I'll go," she says.

When she's halfway down the path toward the gate, I call out, "Stay for a cuppa."

———

Inside, I'm keenly aware of the way Jules takes everything in. She's eyeing the place so methodically I worry for a second that she's casing it to come back later. It's another example of what Ms. Patterson says I tend to do—project onto others what I might do or feel. There was a time when I broke into this very house in order to steal a few things. I didn't think Shay would mind, really. I was nearing rock bottom and just needed one more hit before I gave the old self-detox another go.

Turned out I wasn't alone in the house at the time, though. His girl, Jessica, was in the shower as I was rummaging through the closet. She scared the shite out of me and I lashed out, telling her some cruel things that had nothing to do with any kind of reality. I had never met her, so there was no reason for me to be casting any kind of judgment on her. But I don't always think things through, and I certainly don't have presence of mind when I'm in need of a high.

Shay had come home in the middle of that and nearly broke my neck pushing me out of the room and down the stairs. He was protecting his girl. Not that I had any intention of hurting her, but I guess she was more scared than I was, and he had his priorities.

"So, you're here on your own?" she asks.

"No, I'm not on my own," I say and pause for effect. It works because her eyes widen. I tell her, "I've got Roscoe. He's my partner."

She laughs with relief. "Your brother doesn't live here anymore? Is that what you said?"

I can't help but be suspicious with her bringing up Shay. If I stopped to think about it, I might realize this is normal conversation. A routine kind of getting-to-know-you back and forth. But I don't do that.

"What did the Rogue fan site say? Surely you already know the answer." My voice is a taunt, ready for battle.

"Oh, for fuck's sake," she says with a sigh. "Okay, yes, I know he moved to bloody San Francisco. Yes, I spent some time catching up on all that's happened with the band over the years. But it was really just to see if I could find out more about you. God knows why, but I'm attracted to you. I do have my limits on just how many times I'll have to try to prove that to you, though."

"I just . . . I just don't get it. *Why* do you like me?" *If it's truly nothing to do with McManus?* I add to myself.

"You're a good lay."

I nod in agreement and wait for more.

67

"You're funny. You like dogs."

"And what more? What is it that brought you here?"

Jules glances around the room as if she'll find her answer in the things there. But it's just a sitting room with comfortable furniture and a cold fireplace.

"I need a real answer," I tell her. Even if she says she's here because she wants to get close to Gavin and Rogue again, at least I'll respect the honesty of that. But what she says is more honest than anything I could have imagined.

"Because I'm fucked up," she says. "And you're fucked up. Not in the same way, but still, I see something of me in you. I feel like we could give each other something. Even if it's just taking the edge off this loneliness we both feel."

14

For once in my life, I exercise restraint and call Gavin before driving over to his grand estate in Dalkey, the coastal refuge for Ireland's cultural elite. He and Conor each have homes overlooking the Irish Sea, the likes of which could be featured in one of those fancy architectural magazines. At least Shay hasn't gotten so far up his own arse that he'd get an ostentatious show of wealth like these guys. Though I have to admit the car I've borrowed from him is a show of that.

I have no idea if Gavin is home when I get to his gate. See, even though I phoned him, he didn't answer. I couldn't hold back from forcing the issue, so Roscoe and I hopped in the Porsche and headed over.

It's a brilliant, sunny day. The bright light has turned the water a stunning deep green and steady winds have brought ripples of whitecaps to the surface. This is the view Gavin has from inside his home, and after I get lost in it for a moment, I realize the seductive pull of it. Especially on a rare clear day like today. There's no more beautiful spot on earth than the Irish coastline when the sun is shining down on it. No wonder the bastard lives here.

After ringing the intercom, I get a quick response from the lady of the house, Sophie. She doesn't question my unannounced appearance, but rather invites me to drive through the gate she's remotely opened. I can't say I'm surprised by the welcome. Though I don't know her well, Sophie has always been kind to me, even during those times in the past when I was strung out and probably alarmed her. And she's been especially welcoming of me in the last year since I've been a steady presence with the band.

At the door, Sophie greets me with a smile. She's wearing a delicate white linen top under a rose colored knitted cardigan that would have made anyone else look grandmotherly. But she's paired it with blue jeans that mold to her thin, shapely legs, and besides that, she's a supermodel who has been on more high-end international fashion magazine covers than just about anyone you can think of. She'd make a burlap sack look good.

"Come in," she tells me. "Hi Roscoe."

Thankfully, she and the guys of the band have all accepted Roscoe. He's a good dog who keeps to himself whenever we're out or at someone else's house. Their home is one of those places you instantly feel comfortable in. It's warm and well-designed without being untouchable. They really live in the space.

"Sorry to disturb," I tell her, looking around for signs of Daisy. Their daughter Daisy must be about a year old now. She's all Gavin could talk about when we were on tour.

"Gavin was getting Daisy to nap," Sophie says, "when he fell asleep, too."

"Oh, so he's down for the count?"

"No, he's waking up. I told him you were here. He'll be out in a minute."

I nod, and she sets me up in the kitchen breakfast nook with the promise of a cuppa while I wait. Roscoe leans against my leg before sitting on my feet. Sophie doesn't make small talk, and usually I feel the need to disturb the quiet. But for the moment, I enjoy just watching her. She moves fluidly around the kitchen, preparing the tea like a native rather than the transplant American that she is. I wasn't around when she was here initially as a sixteen-year-old doing a year of school abroad. I'd started on my party crowd life of hopping around Europe by then and didn't pay much attention to what was happening back home. In the years that followed, I gleaned as much as the average observer, which is to say, there was no way I couldn't know just about every detail of the great Gavin and Sophie romance. They have been *the* tabloid couple to command the world's attention for a dozen years. That attention only intensified during their separation and the near end of their marriage a few years back and continues to this day.

All that comes to mind as I watch Sophie. She's not only beautiful, but so clearly the right match for Gavin. They may have had their troubles, but they're one of those couples you could never imagine not lasting. This certainty was one of the reasons why I let go some of my suspicions of Jules yesterday when she showed up at my house. Because, I thought, if she was really after some sort of connection with Gavin again, she'd surely never get far. Gavin and Sophie are too solid for anything to take them down.

"Aye, DB," Gavin says breezily as he comes into view.

"DB" is his nickname for me, shortening Danny Boy. It's one of the character traits I hate about Gavin. He's forever ingratiating himself with people by giving them nicknames they didn't ask for. Well, let me amend that. He long ago started calling Shay by the full, proper name of Seamus. It's what our parents were too lazy to start with as they jumped straight to the nickname instead. I never thought to call him Seamus, but Gavin doing so seems to please the kid and I can't fault that.

"Hey, Gav." I don't bother to get up to greet the guy since he's gone to kiss his wife before helping her bring the tea to the table and settling in.

"Seamus know you're driving his Porsche?" he asks as he gives Roscoe a pat.

"What else am I going to drive?"

"Maybe not the million-dollar sports car. But that's between you two," he says with a smile. "What brings you 'round?" he asks.

"I'll let you two talk," Sophie says.

While Gavin and I have been having this idle chatter, Sophie has been setting out a bowl of water for Roscoe along with a plate of scraps she pulled from the refrigerator. She and Shay are similar in that they are the type of caretakers that are always anticipating others' needs.

I watch as Gavin grabs her hand when she starts to go. She looks down at him with a smile that conveys something private, something only the two of them understand. It's their intimacy on display and I'm struck by a sense of longing for that same kind of deep connection.

"Thanks for the tea, Sophie," I tell her.

She gives me a smile, too, but it's not the same. Damn, she makes me wonder what that kind of love is like.

"Everything okay with your brother?" Gavin asks once Sophie's gone.

"Em, yeah. At least I should think so. He's cleaning up that mess with Marty, though, isn't he?"

Gavin laughs, amused by his band mate's folly. "I suppose he is."

"Remember when you used to be the interesting one?" I ask, thinking of his scandals, including family troubles, a stripper's claims at having bedded him, and a public cocaine problem. "Now you're taking naps with a toddler like an old man."

That gets another laugh out of him. "I'll tell you, I quite like being the boring one. But I won't cop to being old. I was just tired from a rough night."

"Everything okay?"

He hesitates, which is unusual. Jules was on to something when she said I reminded her of Gavin. Neither of us speak with a filter. Gavin does the same thing in his song lyrics. He's always had the charm to take the edge off the brutal honesty that comes from this. That's where he and I differ. My takes are usually just seen as offensive.

"Yeah, it's all grand now," he finally says. "It was something that got me called down to Rosslare. I didn't get home until late, so I've been catching up on sleep."

With that, he puts an end to the explanation by picking up his mug of tea and taking a sip. He's in an oddly introspective mood and I question whether I should move forward with my plan. That better judgment doesn't last long, though. It never does.

"So, I've come 'round to get your impression on something," I say. "Or, *someone*, really."

"Who would that be?"

"A friend of yours from back in the day. A woman named Jules O'Flaherty."

Gavin seems slow to register the name. It must be the lack of sleep. But now that I really look at him, I see he's more than just tired. There's an uncommon weariness about him that I suspect he brought back with him from Rosslare.

"You do know her?" I prod.

It takes one more beat, but finally, he clears his throat, drinks more tea, and nods. "Yeah, but haven't had any real contact with her in years. What's the story?"

"That's what I came to ask you. See, I met her the other day and it came up that she knew you. I'm curious if there's anything I should know about her."

"Jules . . . what can I tell you about Jules? Well, she's a true tough Northside girl, for one." He laughs softly, staring out at the sea view for a moment, lost in thought.

"You had a thing with her? Like, you were with her?"

"Eh, yeah. Once upon a time."

"Before Sophie?"

"Yes, before Sophie and I got back together for good. Jules was a singer, coming up at the same time as us. Had a good voice but didn't really have the will to stick with it. She wanted success but not all the bullshit that goes into getting it."

Jules' musical ambition—or lack thereof—is less important to me than what I ask next. "Why didn't you two make it?"

"Make it?" Gavin gives me a perplexed face before sorting it out. "Oh, you mean as a couple? I dunno." He rubs his face roughly, fighting off a yawn. "We were just having a good time, I thought. Being young and pursuing music and all that. I never fell in love. She might have. But then we went our separate ways—her to tour Europe and us to tour America. That's when I reconnected with Sophie, and I never looked back."

"How'd she take that?"

"Not well at first. But pretty quickly she realized Sophie wasn't going anywhere. We got back into friend mode. She was around at parties and hanging out in the studio when we recorded. It was fine."

That sounds so inconsequential. But based on the number of times Jules has brought up Gavin's name since I met her, I know there's more to it.

"What else, though?" I ask. "Is there more to your history?"

After a moment of contemplation, Gavin laughs and says, "Well, there was the one time she almost got me divorced."

"What was that about?"

Gavin goes on to tell me that though he and Jules reestablished their friendship after he and Sophie were reunited, Jules always seemed to be angling to make it into something more. That included the time she stayed the night at Gavin's place when Sophie was out of town. Sophie had been doing a Sports Illustrated photoshoot at some far flung tropical location, which delayed her getting back to Dublin. Gavin admits he was angry that she had changed their plans of a reunion since it had been weeks since they'd been together. So, when Jules showed up at his house, he was ready for her company— even a little eager for the opportunity to make Sophie jealous.

"We were still young," Gavin explains. Then he laughs. "Or at least young enough. I was aiming to hurt Sophie without really committing any sin. And Jules was game. There's no doubt in my mind she would have helped me cheat on Sophie. But it didn't happen. We just stayed up most the night listening to music and smoking weed and drinking. I fell asleep sitting on the floor up against the sofa. When I woke, Jules had curled up next to me, her head on my chest. And her hand on my cock."

At this, I look away from Gavin and around the open floorplan of the house. Never one to hold back out of any sense of decorum, I now find myself in the unusual position of worrying what effect

Gavin's words might have on someone else. But Sophie is nowhere to be found and I relax a degree.

"This stuff—Sophie doesn't know it," Gavin said. "She doesn't know that Jules tried to fuck me that morning. Or that I shut it down and we each cooled off with a shower. In separate bathrooms. What Sophie knows is that when she came home not long after that, Jules was in our kitchen cooking me breakfast as if we *had* just been shagging all morning. My brilliant idea to make Sophie jealous worked and nearly fucked everything up. It would take a whole lot more down the line to really tear us apart, but we survived that episode."

I'm not quite sure what to say about this revelation.

"So, why did I tell you this intimate thing, you wonder?" Gavin asks with a wry smile. "Because you asked me what you should know about Jules. I have plenty of other stories—other times when she was happy to insert herself between me and Sophie, times when she latched onto Rogue's success, times when she fed me coke as I was trying to quit." He stops and takes a breath before leaning forward against the table and looking me in the eyes. There's focus in his expression now. "It all comes down to this: she's an opportunist. She'll always do what's good for her. So, watch your fucking back."

15

This warning surprises me. Not because I had dismissed all such thoughts about Jules, but because Gavin is so firm in the declaration. He's not known to drop friends easily. Hell, he's *still* best friends with Conor Quinn, even after Quinn had an affair with Sophie. So, for Gavin to disavow Jules is something.

I want to ask a million questions, but Daisy has woken from her nap and is taking drunken steps toward us, her blonde hair a bedhead scramble. Sophie trails behind her, letting the kid be independent but still close enough to catch her if she falls.

When Gavin see his daughter, his blue eyes widen and light up. The smile on his face is pure joy and almost changes my mind about not wanting kids. I've never had that desire. And even if I did, I'd probably still choose not to have kids. Not when I know how easy it is to fuck them up, which I'd surely do.

Gavin gets up and meets Daisy halfway, encouraging her to keep walking. She lets out a squeal and moves faster when he goes down onto his knees. Soon, she's flying into his waiting arms.

I'm no stranger to intruding upon others' domestic bliss—doing so is what got me and Shay those decent meal from our neighbors a few times a week when we were kids—but I figure I can't talk to Gavin about what I really want to with his wife and daughter in the mix, and so Roscoe and I take off.

Before I go, however, I extract from Gavin the promise not to tell Shay about this. I argue that even though there's nothing there with Jules, that wouldn't stop Shay from worrying about it. Thankfully, Gavin agrees that there's no need to stir things up for the kid.

I find myself doing as Shay does when he's got something on his mind: driving.

I've never been into cars, but the Porsche is a fun machine. It responds to the slightest maneuvering, making you feel like you're powerful and in full control. Must be why Shay likes these things so much. As kids, we had zero control over our lives. We were just fighting for survival.

My directionless driving takes us east on M50 before turning southward onto N81. The day is still gorgeous, even as I trade Gavin's sea view for the rural countryside of County Wicklow. I pull through the town of Blessington and figure it's a good time for a pint. Murphy's Pub right on Main Street does the trick.

I seem to have hit the old folks' hour as there's a group of white-haired gents taking up the far side of the bar. They're arguing amongst themselves over which horse to bet on. A race is being broadcast up on one of the three large plasmas on the wall. It's an off time, so it's just me and Roscoe, the bartender, and the old fellas who pay us no mind. Taking a bar stool a few seats from them, I nod to the barman. He's got a mop of curly brown hair graying at the temples and the combination of a protruding belly and skinny legs that seems to afflict certain middle-aged men.

"You bringing that dog in with you?" the barman asks.

"My therapy animal," I reply reflexively. It might as well be true. Roscoe has become an indispensable part of my life. I've just never done any paperwork to prove his value in that regard to others.

The barman seems to consider challenging me on this, but it doesn't last long. His easygoing nature, the thing that's probably made him great at his job for a good number of years, wins out. He shrugs to himself and asks, "What'll it be?"

"Pint."

"Guinness?"

"Is there anything else as fine on God's green earth?"

He tsks in agreement and sets about the long pour in the proper fashion. It'll be ready for me in a few minutes time.

"You here for a drive around the Blessington Lake?" he asks.

"The what?"

The barman goes on to tell me I've stumbled upon one of the hidden glories of not just County Wicklow, but all of Ireland. In fact, famed Irish writer Brendan Behan called it the "jewel of Wicklow." The lake is really a reservoir and has fifty miles of shoreline. The drive around it promises not just views of the water, but of pristine mountainscapes. The barman proudly boasts of the fact that many a film and television show has been produced in this very town, centering on the breathtaking lake and surrounding picturesque villages.

After almost five minutes of this gushing, I say, "For god's sake, do you work for the Irish Tourism Board or what? Can't you just listen to my troubles like a normal barman?"

The fellow laughs ruefully. "I do get excited, especially with the weather so fair. Brings out the poet in me, I suppose." He takes a moment to finish pouring my Guinness before setting it in front me. He then leans his forearm against the end of the bar and gives me his full attention. "Tell me your troubles, son."

"Well, it can't be like that. It's supposed to flow natural like. You're not my fucking priest, are you?"

The barman sighs in agreement rather than frustration. "Right you are. Let me just check on the fellas at the end there and I'll be back."

I take a good long pull on the Guinness and it goes down lovely as can be. And I wonder what Jules is doing all alone where I left her in Shay's house.

16

Jules' declaration that we were some kind of magic match for each other because we are both fucked up had left me speechless. I'm aware enough to understand I've always been attracted to women who have their own issues but being called out on it so blatantly threw me. She was bluntly suggesting we acknowledge our shortcomings and that that acceptance of one another would be something unique we could get from no one else.

My answer had been no answer at all. Instead, I pulled her to me and kissed her with such intensity and desperation that I was close to tears over the torturous feeling of it. That didn't stop me, of course, from fucking her right there in the sitting room. And then again upstairs in my room. And finally, once again in the Man Cave after spending a good part of the night drinking Jameson, playing snooker, and trying to keep her off Shay's drum kit.

I left her sleeping on the sofa in order to go talk to Gavin.

I laugh softly to myself sitting here in this pub thinking of the fact that she still doesn't have my cell number. There was no reason to exchange numbers when we were naked in each other's company.

"Another, then?" the barman asks with a nod toward my nearly empty pint glass.

"Ay."

While waiting for the Guinness to settle, the barman takes another stab at being the kind of sounding board people in his profession usually are.

"And so, what brings you our way?" he asks.

"Just out for a drive. Needed to clear my head a bit," I admit.

"Let me guess—problems to do with the female persuasion?"

"You could say that. It's complicated."

"I've heard all kind of things in my day. Give me a try."

"How about this one: the girl I'm sleeping with used to be with a mate of mine. That mate just told me the girl is trouble. She seems like no more trouble that the average woman. But do I take his word and move on? Or do I stick it out and see for myself, whatever the consequences?"

The barman lets out a low whistle as he ponders my predicament. "Well, the expression 'plenty of fish in the sea' came about for a reason. Unless this girl is your one? Like the song goes?"

Jesus, Mary, and Joseph. The man is quoting a Rogue song to me. "You're My One" was their runaway smash hit off their second album. It propelled them to worldwide fame. It was so big they could have quit and lived happily off the royalties of that one song. That's great for them, but it's meant that the song has become a cultural fixture. You still hear it at least once a day on the radio in the shops. And yokes like this barman quote it as if it's some sort of Shakespearean sonnet.

Just to grate on my nerves even more, the barman starts humming the song before launching into a passionate rendering of the lyrics, "My heart, that feral bird, has found the sky in your eyes."

"Ah, I just love that part. Speaks to my love of nature and my love of love," the barman says.

"Fuck's sake, man," I tell him. "Get it together. I'm not in love with this woman. I'm only trying to figure out if I should even give it a chance."

"Always give love a chance, that's what I say."

I suspect this guy's lady gave him a wake-up blowjob this

morning but stop myself from saying so. No one has the right to be this happy, this positively *giddy*, over the mere idea of love.

"Thanks very much," I say. When he finally passes me my second pint, I turn away enough to give him the hint that I'm done asking for his advice.

———

After the barman's sales pitch, there's no way I can't do the drive around the lake. Roscoe and I make the journey, stopping where possible at inlets and chatting with fisherman on a catch and release mission for coarse and pike. It's as stunning as advertised. And peaceful, too. It gives me the space to think through what I want with Jules.

What I realize is that the warning I got about her is the exact type of thing someone would say of me. Meaning, Jules is right. We're both fucked up. And we'll be judged for that by anyone who knows us. So, why not see what we can be together?

And if that ends up being trouble, well, it won't be the first time.

17

Jules is nowhere to be found when Roscoe and I get back to the house. And because I'm a dope and don't have her cell number either, we get back into the car and head to her place.

I spot her car out front and hear music inside, so I know she's home. But she doesn't answer my knock. Being a persistent bastard, I keep up with the tapping until she's forced to come to the door. She's just out of the shower with wet hair and in a robe, looking exasperated.

"Danny Boy, what do you want?"

"Ah, no. That's not the game we're playing, love," I tell her as Roscoe and I head inside. Roscoe makes for Molly—and her food dish—out on the patio.

Resigned, Jules shuts the door, folds her arms across her chest, and stares at me.

"You came 'round to my place last night unannounced with a bit of a proposition. I never did answer you, though, did I?"

She cocks her head and does her best to act disinterested. This tells me she's none too pleased that I ditched her earlier. I hadn't expected to be gone for quite as long as I was, but I know that excuse won't help me here.

"Problem is, you were too fucking sexy for me to keep my hands to myself," I say, hoping to win her over with flattery.

"Get to your point," she says, clearly unimpressed.

"My point, Jules, is that I think you're right about us. About who we are and what we can get from each other. So, yeah. Let's be fucked up together and see how it goes."

There's a smile at her lips that she's trying to hold back. But it disappears once I keep talking.

"Just one condition."

"Oh, there's a condition?"

"Let this be about *us*. I don't want to hear Gavin fucking McManus' name from you again."

She lifts her chin and straightens her back. For a moment I think she's going to argue against this. But then she goes in the opposite direction and I breathe a sigh of relief.

"Perfectly fine with me," she says.

———

So, there it is. We've decided to . . . what? Be in a relationship? Neither of us really has the answer to that. This grand little moment of me showing up to say we should be together suddenly turns awkward as we watch each other expectantly.

"Well," I start but say no more.

"Em, yeah. Right," she agrees.

After a pause, we both laugh.

"Drink?" she asks.

And so it begins. This is how we will ease into our fucked-up connection.

"Let's do," I say and watch as she moves toward the kitchen.

This reliance on drink feels all too familiar. This is all I've ever done with women. Usually it jumps very quickly from alcohol to heroin, but even though Jules and I skip the H, it still feels like the same thing. Ms. Patterson would call it my *pattern of avoidance*. In other words, I have always used substances as a way to dodge mean-ingful relationships—with others, with myself, blah blah blah.

I do that because it feels good. It's what my comfort level is. I've long known that if both the woman I'm with and I are medicated with booze or smack, then nothing can really hurt. I won't ever really feel insecure or disappointed or unwanted. I've plunged into this way of existence so many times before that it's easy to see why it is so natural this time.

Only, something *is* different this time. Now, I've got Ms. Patter-son's voice in my head. It's crowding out all the other ones that tell me I deserve nothing good. It's pointing out that I'm endangering the progress I've made. It's urging me to break the mold.

"Hold up," I tell her as she reaches for a whiskey bottle in the kitchen cabinet.

She looks at me and waits.

"Mightn't I take you out? On a date, like?"

The idea is as preposterous to her as it is to me. That's not what this was supposed to be. But I can't let it go on as she proposed—two fuck-ups giving into, and maybe even exacerbating, their deficien-cies. After twenty odd years of living the fucked-up way, I'm surprised to find that I want to at least try something different.

After a moment, she reconsiders her reaction and her features soften. A smile brightens her face. "That's very gallant of you. In fact, me hanging out with grungy musicians pretty much all my life has meant no one has ever really taken me on a proper date."

The fact that I've never once taken a woman out on a proper date either doesn't stop me from saying, "That's a sin, isn't it?"

She laughs, and it comes out girlish, charmed. And it makes me want to wow her. Maybe this could be something real.

———

We split up with the agreement that I'll return for her at seven o'clock. First thing I do is get my hair cut and have a shave. The barber transforms me from Scooby Doo's mate Shaggy into a poor man's Christian Bale. That's an improvement, by the way.

Next, Roscoe and I head home for a bit of internet research. I struggle to think of what people do on a date. Typing in the search engine, "where to go for a night out in Dublin" brings me a million suggestions for pubs. Again, with the drink. Jesus, is that all people do?

I sit back and try to think. What's it supposed to be about? Getting to know each other, right? Well, what do I already know about Jules? She's a burned-out singer. She's a feminist. She's some sort of artist. That sparks an idea and I type again into the search engine.

After several misses, I find the right option. There's an art gallery in Temple Bar offering a talk this very evening. A visiting artist named Cassandra McMackin is speaking about the portrayal of women in art from the second world war to the present. Not exactly something I'd rush to on my own, but it sounds perfect for Jules. That and a spot of dinner afterward has got to be the makings of a proper date.

I've got just enough time to take a shower and dress before I have to be back at Jules'. My normal gear doesn't seem up to snuff for the evening, so I help myself to Shay's closet. I used to be a lot skinnier than him, but my healthy ways have seen me fill out my frame to good effect. I've even acquired some toned muscles thanks to all my wanderings with Roscoe. I'm definitely the taller of the two of us brothers, but I manage to find something of Shay's that works: new black jeans I fold at the cuffs to disguise that they're a bit too short, a black silk long sleeve shirt, and a three-quarters length dark gray tailored coat that fits just right. The coat is lightweight and has black accents on the collar and lapels. I check the tag and see it's Tom Ford. It would be too big on Shay, but damn if it doesn't work perfectly for me.

Surveying myself in the mirror, I'm impressed as fuck. Doesn't take much to get me looking good.

Roscoe and I make a quick stop at a Marks & Spencer on the way over to pick up flowers. I grab yellow daisies because they're a happy color. No need to get as serious as red roses.

At Jules' house, my attempt to get Roscoe to hold the flowers between his jaws as a cute gesture fails and I'm left gripping the slobber coated plastic wrapping.

The effort Jules has made to pretty herself up doesn't go lost on me when she opens the door. She's done her hair, and it's the first time I've seen her wear makeup, let alone a dress. The teal strapless dress hugs her body and goes well with her tattoos. The stuff she did her blue eyes with makes them pop. And I'm tempted to suck the plum color lipstick right off her. She's gorgeous and I tell her so.

"You're looking transformed yourself," she says. "It's *good.*"

I nod my thanks and offer her the flowers. "Sorry, the wrapping is a bit dodgy. Roscoe had a chew."

She gingerly takes the flowers and tells me to come in so she can put them in water before we go. Because she has the covered patio and Roscoe and Molly get on so well, we'd already planned to leave the dogs at her place. Once they're settled, Jules grabs her purse and a wrap and we're off.

"Are we really driving in this?" she asks as I open the passenger door of the Porsche for her.

"It's the only ride I've got," I tell her. "It'll be fine."

When I'm on my side, I look over at her and see she's sunk into the bucket seat and eyeing all the gadgetry of the panels.

"Don't worry," I say, "it's just a car."

"A very expensive car."

I start the engine and look over at her.

"I came across all the tabloid stories about Shay's extravagant purchase when I was trying to see where he lived," she explains.

"Good thing I know how to drive it, then isn't it?" I don't want to go back into that whole thing of her researching Shay and the guys. It was too stalker-ish at the time. Talking more about what else she learned would only add to that feeling.

"Let's see what you can do," she says with a wink and I gladly drive on.

18

"You did an amazing job of appearing interested."

I laugh and shake my head. We've moved on from the art gallery to a highly regarded Tapas place not far from St. Stephens Green.

"I actually was interested," I say. "I mean some of it went over my head, but there was definitely stuff that kept my attention."

Jules leans back against the red pillow of her banquette seat and eyes me for a moment. We're tucked into the corner of the restaurant, next to the front window and under the chalkboard with handwritten specials. The lights are low and with just one small candle between us, it feels comfortably intimate. The awkwardness of us doing things arse over tea kettle by fucking first and dating second has eased off a bit.

"Well, you did good with that choice," she says.

I hold up my glass of Cava Brut. We got a bottle on recommendation from the waiter and are sipping it along with our first round of tapas: plump Malaga olives, Manchego cheese with honey, and deceptively simple bread with bits of tomato and olive oil that is delicious,

"Cheers to that," I tell her. I've justified the wine by the fact that it's with dinner. And it's to be enjoyed, not just a numbing agent. So

91

far, so good on that front. We're both running at the same speed, it seems, as Jules has been nursing her glass the same way I have.

We clink glasses and share a moment in each other's gaze before taking a drink. She's a beauty and I tell her so.

"You're actually pretty good at this dating thing," she says.

I hope she's right. I realize I want desperately for something good to come out of this, to push this into something different and stable. This evening feels like the right start.

I suppose we're to make some get-to-know-you talk, so I say, "You grew up Northside, yeah? How was that?"

She laughs, but this time without any offense. "It was all right. Made me tough, I suppose. That and the fact that I've got two older brothers who loved to torture me."

"How so?"

"Ah, they'd tickle me until I was crying. They'd make up elaborate stories of how I was adopted and that our parents were going to give me back to the orphanage any day. They'd hide my favorite things— dolls when I was little, makeup when I was older. They'd do every-thing they could to scare away boys who liked me."

"The bastards," I say playfully. "I'll fight 'em for you."

"They were just being boys. No real harm. But I think they helped motivate me to spend time in my room with music on, singing right along with Liz Phair, and Fiona Apple, and Dolores of The Cran-berries."

"How did making a real go of it come about?"

Even though she shrugs, her eyes light up. The memory of her early days seems to play in her mind for a moment. I let her get lost in it, content to watch her.

"It was a brief, bright moment," she finally says. "The music scene was hot in Dublin and your brother's band was leading the charge. I saw them play at The Basement. It's this dodgy little club that made a habit of opening up the mics to would-be musicians like them. And like myself. I got up the nerve one night to play acoustic guitar and sing. Caught the notice of the man who would become my manager.

Things moved quickly, as we all went en masse to London to seek out record deals. That's actually where I met—"

She stops herself from saying Gavin's name.

"Anyway, it was the life for a while. I did countless shows all over Europe, made an album, and got enough of a following to be able to keep at it. It lasted for a quite a few years. Girls like me, with an earnest girl power bent, did well for a time. And then the pop shite of groups like the Pussycat Dolls, spouting their sexualized bullshit, took over. It was good while it lasted, but I had no desire to conform to that crap to keep my name known. I opted out rather than play a game where the rules were made to set up ninety-nine percent of people to fail. Make that ninety-nine percent of *women*. Blokes like Rogue did just fine. And so, here I am."

There's bitterness in her voice. And regret. But she is trying to act dismissive of it all, so I let the subject drop. Before I can come up with some amusing remark to lighten things up, our waitress comes loaded down with more to eat.

We've got sautéed lamb sweetbreads, an oxtail casserole, and a squid ink seafood and black rice dish, along with potatoes and red bell peppers. The food presents a time of refuge for us both as we drop talk of Jules' music career and instead take turns sampling each dish and trading our assessment of them. It feels ridiculously pedestrian, like we're an old married couple who after being together forever have nothing left to talk about except for the day's big meal.

And then Jules changes all that by asking, "What made you start heroin?"

19

It's like the proverbial record scratch that dramatically halts all conversation. I lose my appetite and sit back in my chair. We were just talking about Jules and what made her who she is. I had instigated the conversation by asking her about where she grew up, a rather good way to try to understand someone.

She started her own attempt to know me by asking about drugs. For fuck's sake, is that all I am? Is heroin the sum of my parts to anyone else looking at me?

Or is it that Jules is still hoping that I'll be her guide down that path and all this other stuff has been for show?

"I had a shitty childhood, Jules," I tell her with the hope that will end this. To emphasize the point, I drain my wine glass in three gulps and refill it.

"A lot of people did."

"Your point?"

"Just it doesn't always have to go the way it went for you. What was the difference?"

"My therapist's name is Ms. Patterson. Why don't you look her up and have a wee chat about it all if you're so bothered?"

"Don't get so defensive," she says softly, leaning toward me. "You have to have thought about this."

Of course, I have. I've thought about it far more than I want to say. I've wondered why I went that route when Shay was able to live a basically normal life. We both had the same loser parents and god-awful upbringing, but he was able to get through life without the constant negativity in his head dragging him down. He never needed any escape other than music. He ended up with a lovely woman, Jessica, who I'm sure he'll marry and have kids with. I am over the moon that it turned out that way for him. Honest to god, I am. But I do wonder: Why not me?

"I never learned a trade," I say. "Not until I got on tour with my brother and started learning the ins and outs of stage lighting. I mostly do the grunt work, but I've picked up a lot along the way. It's fascinating to see what small adjustments can do for the mood of a show. I'm going to focus on the more technical aspects once they go back out on the road again."

Jules just stares at me. My attempt to change the subject falls flat. But I don't care. If being with her means I have to speak to her like I do Ms. Patterson, complete with all the soul-searching and self-analysis, then I'll be on my merry way. It's far too exhausting doing that with the person being paid to listen, I don't want to do it with the person I'm fucking.

"We about done here?" I ask. I look about for the waiter, despite the fact that half our food has gone untouched.

"You don't want me in your head," she says, as if such a thing is a curiosity.

Looking back at her, I tell her with as much honesty as I can bear, "I want you to separate me from the heroin. When I told you about that I didn't think it'd become this fascination for you. I didn't think it'd be this thing you use to poke and prod me with. I'm doing my best to be fucking done with the stuff. I don't want to talk about it at every turn."

There's a long moment where we watch each other without saying a thing. I'm hoping my expression gets across that I need her to leave this issue alone. Her expression tells me she's weighing whether she can do just that.

Finally, she responds. First, by leaning forward and reaching under the table to touch my knee. In that position, her breasts are pressed together and further exposed in the strapless top of her dress. Her skin is pale and the memory of how soft her nipples feel right before they harden, has me breathing a little faster. Her fingers trail up my inner thigh as far as she can go.

"Give me a two-minute head start," she says, "then meet me in the loo."

Back to sex being our true connection. What man would say no to that?

Certainly not me.

20

Except for when she's got her women's empowerment painting projects, Jules and I play a bit of house together in the next few days. I stay over at her place in the evenings, and it's easy company. I chalk up our date as a fruitless endeavor. It wasn't the start to the good, stable relationship I had the audacity to hope for because Jules can't see me as anything more than the heroin addict I've always been, no matter how hard I want to leave that version of me behind. Maybe that's my fault because I don't want to share with her how it all started for me. But maybe it's her fault because she doesn't want to take the time to see what else I am.

In any case, we've slipped right into the thing I was hoping to avoid. We don't further confront the fact that this connection is born out of something dark and lonely in ourselves. We just medicate it with each other's bodies and companionship. I find it hard to see anything really negative about it. At least I'm not doing H.

But the fact that I say nothing to Shay about her when we speak is revealing in itself. I don't want him to know I've even met Jules, let alone sought out—and disregarded—Gavin's advice about her. Keeping it a secret is a bad idea. It's how things start to slide downhill. At least in my experience it is. I've gone this route before. At first it feels inconsequential. A minor detail that no one else needs to know about. It quickly escalates to rationalizations that can jeopardize everything, like convincing yourself you really do know, *this time*, how to handle heroin.

To balance things out, I vow to tell Ms. Patterson all about it at our Monday session. When we began together, it was with twice-a-week sessions on Mondays and Thursdays, with the plan that we'd cut back to just once per week, but I quickly began to look forward to our time together so much that I'd watch the clock in between appointments. But this time, it feels like an age has passed since I've even thought of Ms. Patterson. Last Thursday's session was when I thought she might be jealous about Jules, when I taunted her a bit over it. And she didn't like it.

In what seems to be a direct response to that, she's buttoned up today. Literally. She's wearing a high collared black blouse that has small buttons up the middle along with black trousers. No more pencil skirts for me, I guess.

She doesn't laugh when I ask her who died. Instead, she places her notepad in her lap and has her pen poised to jot notes.

This promises to yield very little fun. Where is the woman who clearly liked me despite my fuck-ups? The one who joked with me even after I interrupted her dinner date with her girlfriends?

I decide we need to get back to that favorable dynamic.

"I may have a new client for you," I say. "Give you one guess who it might be. Here's a clue: he's very recently been in the tabloids—both times for having his trousers down around his ankles."

"Let's talk about you and not Martin Whelan," she replies without humor.

"You have to admit, it is a wee bit funny, these things he's gotten himself into back-to-back."

I had seen the tabloid news of Martin's latest foray—this time with a groupie right here in Dublin—just yesterday when I was out early in the morning to walk Roscoe. We went past a newsstand and the front-page story was hard to miss. I snatched up a copy and devoured it along with breakfast back at the house.

"I called Shay straightaway," I say. "Woke the kid there in the

States but had to be sure he knew the trouble his mate was getting himself into. Even if it was also a laugh."

Ms. Patterson hasn't budged. She's still a block of ice. Like frozen water, she's contracted into herself to form a solid, impenetrable mass. I'm at a loss for how to get through and back to our old relationship. I panic at the thought that this is how our relationship will be now.

"Fuck, what is this?" I ask. "Are you angry with me?"

This startles her, and her posture loosens the tiniest bit. A crack in the ice.

"No, Daniel. I am not angry with you," she says. "I'm just eager to get on track and talk about you. Martin Whelan's troubles are his own and shouldn't take up time we could be working on you."

"Got it." I pause. "But you did catch the part of how well hung our man is, yeah? That's what you call a silver fucking lining. What a thing to publicize."

Her defrost is now well underway as she raises her hand to her mouth to try to hide a smile. I feel like the weight of the world has lifted from my shoulders. Besides Shay, there's no one more than Ms. Patterson that I want to please.

"So, I guess I'm in a relationship," I say, getting to the admission I'd promised myself I'd make. "With Jules, the Northersider woman from the park."

A moment passes as she takes this in. "I see. And what does a 'relationship' mean for you?"

"I dunno. Just that we're going to spend time together and see where it leads."

"Does that seem quick at all to you?"

"I have no real experience to compare it to, so can't say."

"Have you never been in a relationship before?"

I shrug. Then I open my mouth to tell her about the woman I thought was going to be my life partner, the one who died of an overdose next to me in bed. But I stop short. That woman was someone I'd known for mere weeks, the majority of which was through the filter of heroin. The reason I don't put forth this story as an example of a relationship—something I've had no problem doing in the past, even to my own brother—is because Ms. Patterson has been making a concerted effort in these sessions to get me to separate reality from fantasy. I've spent basically the last twenty years concocting versions of my life that aren't exactly true. I got so good at it that I've convinced myself some things were true when it was really all a fabrication. But it's how I've been able to avoid dealing with a lot of shit over the years, including the chaos in my head. Most of my bullshit has been harmless, just spouting off to either get a reaction to amuse myself or shaping a story in a way that benefits me somehow. Ms. Patterson argues, though, that it has robbed me of authentic experiences. She says it's meant I'm not actually participating in my own life when I spend all my time looking for the angle, strategizing on how to spin the story into something different. This didn't exactly ring false, and after I let it sink in a bit, I agreed to try to consciously look at things with a view to what is real.

That's what Ms. Patterson was so intent on me sorting out when I stormed in on her dinner date. She told me a few times to look at what had *really* happened, that the version of things I was suggesting where she was having a laugh at my expense wasn't the real one. I came to see that, but only when it was too late. Our "work" here is to get me to the point where I make the right decisions at the right time.

"Well," she says, "why don't you tell me more about your girlfriend. You said she's a housepainter?"

"Nah. Turns out I got that wrong." I tell her all about Jules' mission with her painting and boosting women's self-esteem.

"That's an interesting endeavor."

"I suppose. Doesn't do much for me."

"It's interesting in that you might say she's helping these women discover their sense of identity."

I blow right past that insight, saying, "Maybe so. More power to her and all that. Like I said, it's hard to get all worked up about it. Especially knowing what her real source of income is."

That intrigues Ms. Patterson. She looks up from the notes she had been making and watches me expectantly.

"She used to be a singer. Julia O'Flaherty is her name. Was a decent act back in the day when Rogue was getting up and running, too. I wouldn't know. I was in . . . Italy? I don't know. Somewhere like that. Anyway, turns out she and your man Gavin McManus had a thing. They were together for a time."

"Small world," she muses.

"Is it, though?" I can't help but ask. "I wonder about that sometimes. Anyway, Jules did pretty well for herself. Had three albums. Did a single with McManus. But she's been out of the industry for a while. Still does all right with the royalties from all that."

"How does Gavin feel about you seeing her?"

"Why should he care? Married with a kid and all? It's been *years* since he's even seen her."

"Okay, then it's no problem to bring her around with you."

"Well, I'm happy to keep things quiet for the time being, actually. There's no need to shout this from the rooftops."

She eyes me for a long moment. "What does Shay think?"

"Haven't had a chance to tell him. And not sure I need to rush to that either. The kid's got plenty to deal with now. I don't want him to worry about this."

"Why would he worry about this? If what you say is true—that there are no concerns with her being in the picture."

"Because that's what he does. He worries. And sure, I've given him a million legitimate reasons to worry, but this isn't something he needs to take on. I've got it covered."

21

That's what I truly believe: that I have it covered. Even as over the course of the next few weeks, I fall deeper into dependence on Jules. She's like a drug to me. I can't get enough of her and she seems to feel the same way. It's exactly what both Ms. Patterson and NA warn against—that a relationship too soon in the recovery process can become a substitute for drugs, therefore jeopardizing the path I'm trying to forge. But just like every other time I've slipped, I convince myself that it's different. That I can handle it. I've got it covered.

For her part, Jules is good on her promise and never once mentions Gavin or even Rogue again. That fear of mine—that she's got ulterior motives—fades away. In its place is the gnawing worry that she's pulling me toward the life I've been trying to leave behind. We go to parties together with people she doesn't know well, but yet insists on attending. She likes to smoke weed at these gatherings and is relentless in wanting me to join her even though I've explained more than once that marijuana is the one drug that—paradoxically—amplifies the chaos in my head rather than letting me escape it. We drink too much when we're together. But we also laugh a lot. And fuck a lot. The good feelings outweigh the bad. That's what I tell myself.

———

Then things get dicey one night when Jules drags me out with her to a club in Temple Bar. It's for her friend Jacob who is re-opening the place after a fire had shut it down. She's keen that we show our support. Our presence doesn't matter all that much for most of the night as the specially advertised 2-for-1 drinks fill the place beyond capacity.

When the crowds thin out as it gets close to two in the morning, Jules leaves me in the booth we'd been sharing with Jacob and a few others, so she can go to the ladies.

Jacob is a Scot with a heavy accent, rail-thin, pale, and has a recently shaved head. He's telling me all about how much he misses the shoulder-length dreadlocks he used to have.

"I gave 'em up for someone who ended up leaving me not long after," he moans. "The bitch of it is, they had always said it was my bleedin' *signature*. And now, it's like I'm missing an *essential* part of me."

It's clear enough to me that Jacob's gay, but I'll go ahead and play along with his non-specific pronouns since he doesn't want to be out about it.

"They should never try to change who you are, mate," I tell him. I'm not at all invested in propping up the guy, but it's an amusing way to pass the time at the moment. "If they really liked you to begin with."

This resonates for him as he watches me and nods slowly. But then his eyes go a little glassy. Turns out he's not so much agreeing with me as he is drunk.

"Aye, Jacob," one of his buddies says, "remember when we had a laugh and cut off McManus' hair?"

That perks him up and he smiles wanly. "That was fucking epic."

"Gavin McManus, I suppose?" I ask, though I know the answer.

Dublin is such a small fucking city. All roads lead back to Gavin or Conor or Rogue. People glommed onto them with maybe even more ferocity than their success warranted as a way to give U2 the finger. That band has been lovingly hated for so many years that when Rogue came up, it was as if Dubliners were happy to turn their backs on them by giving all their attention to Rogue.

"Yeah, that cocksucker," Jacob says, slurring the words. Then he laughs, starring at some middle-distance. "At least I hoped he was."

I don't know what the fuck that means but I can't be bothered to ask. Not when I have Jules returning to us, all bright-eyed and practically vibrating from the inside out. She promptly sits on my lap and kisses me.

If I didn't know from her appearance alone, I know from the taste in her mouth as she kisses me that she's just done cocaine. It's a peculiar sour, sweet, salty flavor that is reminiscent of medicine, but yet unlike anything you've ever gotten over the counter. I don't get enough from her, though, to feel that numbness that comes with having rubbed it directly on the gums.

What I do get is pissed off. I push her off me and stand while wiping at my mouth. That doesn't work to take that tempting taste out of my mouth and so I spit on the floor.

"Danny—" Jules starts.

"Fuck off," I say. "This is not cool. You know I can't be around this shit."

"It's nothing," she says. "It was the tiniest taste. I barely even feel it."

"Oh, is it time for that?" Jacob asks with a grin. He ignores the tension and pulls a baggie of white powder out of his pocket and his friends at the booth all move closer to him.

"Not for me," I say. "I'm out of here."

"Come on, don't be that way," Jules says. "It's harmless, really."

I pull up the sleeve of my thermal shirt and slap my inner elbow. The tender skin is marked by a series of small scars. "Go on and stick the needle in for me while you're at it. Is this where we're headed? This what you want, Jules?"

It's a dramatic gesture but it goes unnoticed as the group at the table focuses on the lines being cut and passed around. I'm not surprised at the lack of response to my outburst. They've all got their priorities, too lured in by the prospect of getting high to bother with me, including Jules, who glances at me, then back at the cocaine.

That's answer enough, and I turn and make for the door. Roscoe is at Jules' place. I don't have a key, so I'm distracting myself with thoughts of how I'll jump the wall to her back patio to get him when someone grabs my arm and tugs so hard that I'm spun around.

Jules has caught up to me just outside the club.

"I'm sorry, babe," she says. "I wasn't thinking. I'm so sorry."

There are tears in her eyes. This throws me. I know we have this weird, dependent connection, but I hadn't thought it got to any kind of emotional level. It's felt like we've been using each other more than anything else, but with us each understanding that that is what's going on so it doesn't feel dirty. It was comfortable. It's what got us through the otherwise lonely nights.

"I'm so sorry," she says again. Now the tears fall down her cheeks and she lets them. "I love you. I don't want to hurt you."

Fuck. She *loves* me? I don't know what to do with that. I can't return those words to her. My lack of a response hangs awkwardly in the air as the rain comes down on us.

"Just—just kiss me," she says desperately.

She's giving me an out. It's the out we always take when things get too deep.

And like the addict that I am, I fucking take it.

I pull her to me and kiss her, trying to ignore the faint trace of coke in her mouth and instead concentrate on the way her tits press against me. I know she'll be revved up to fuck because she's high. She'll feel that need. It'll amplify the experience for her. I've been there and done that. I should know better than to enable this. I do know better.

Still, that doesn't stop me.

We get as far as the Porsche before I let it escalate. Luckily, we're parked in a darkened patch of the street around the corner from the club, so when Jules straddles me I don't think twice about someone else seeing us. The light rain and our body heat fogging up the windows helps shield us from passersby.

She's kissing me frantically, grinding on me to the point of it hurting. She can't help herself.

I grab her hips to still her and she looks at me in surprise, her chest heaving.

"Take off your top," I tell her, and she smiles.

The top and bra fly off as I work to unbutton my jeans from under her. She's got on a skirt and the knickers are easy enough to push to the side. As my cock slides into her, I think about the fact that this is the first time we've had sex without a condom. The feeling of her without anything between us makes me moan.

"Tell me you love me," she breathes. "Tell me."

I ignore her and bury my face in her chest, taking her nipple into my mouth as she rides me hard. She's immune to the pressure of my teeth as I bite her tender skin. She doesn't mind when I grip her ass so firmly that I'm sure I'm leaving marks. She's not just riding me. She's riding the high.

Once again, I hold her hips still to get her attention. She looks at me, pained at the prospect of stopping at this moment.

"Is this me you want?" I ask.

"It's you I love," she says.

"Say my name." I allow her the slightest movement against me, tilting her hips forward so her clit gets the good action.

"Danny fucking Boy," she says with a laugh.

Releasing her hips, I move my hands to her tits, squeezing them with satisfaction. She doesn't move, though. She's waiting for my command.

"Go on. Come for me. But don't stop until you've got my every last drop."

That's what she wanted. As much as she is a feminist and wants to be in control of her life, I've found she loves to be told what to do in bed. Or in the car, as the case may be. She does as she's told and we both find the delicious distraction we were after.

———

There's no acknowledgement by either of us the next morning of what went on the night before. We don't talk about her doing cocaine or how she tried to dismiss it. We don't talk about her saying she loves me. Or how I didn't return the sentiment.

We do acknowledge the amazing sex in the car, though. That's when Jules lets me know she's on birth control. I'm relieved to hear that. We joke about where we might get our freak on next, since we've now done it in both a restaurant toilet and a car.

"Maybe we should take a trip somewhere, just so we can try out the mile-high club," she says with a devilish grin.

"Where would we go?"

My question turns this hypothetical into something more, and we spend the good part of the day brainstorming and looking up places on the internet. Jules steers us toward higher-end hotels or resorts in each location, making me realize how quickly she's shed all that Northsider holier-than-thou bullshit she espoused when we first met. In fact, she's embraced my "poncy Southsider" lifestyle quite easily. She likes when we drive the Porsche. She likes when we stay in Shay's luxurious house.

I hadn't thought very much about the progression of all that until now. A warning bell goes off in my head. It's the worry that her flipping so quickly means she's using me.

Rather than confront this, I decide one way to test how tied she is to these material things is to get my own mode of transportation. For reasons I don't quite understand, I reach out to Conor Quinn to assist me. He got a motorbike not long ago and I ask him if he'll lend me his expertise and show me some of the basics to see if it's something I might want to invest in. His ego suitably stroked, Mr. Perfect, agrees.

22

Ye meet on a Sunday morning in Sandyford Industrial Estate to take advantage of the quiet streets of the business park there. Conor's waiting when I arrive, decked out in dark jeans with his usual silver pocket chain, biker boots, and a black and red leather jacket that conforms to his broad chest. Mirrored sunglasses cover his eyes, and yet I can sense his amusement as I step out of the Porsche. I'm in my usual gear—old jeans with suspenders and a stretched-out tee shirt over a thermal.

I don't often feel inadequate in comparison to other people because I learned long ago that I'd really be fucked if I started that. It was always a better plan to not care how I rated against others, to just do my own thing and be my own person. I'm successful at this most of the time. But whenever I'm near Conor, all that disappears. He's better looking, smarter, more confident, more accomplished, and just generally a step above most everyone else—and that definitely includes me. It's no secret that's why he irritates me so much. All those feelings rush forward now as I join him at his bike, and I wonder why the fuck I thought asking him to lord his knowledge over me was a good idea.

"Hey man," he says with a nod.

"Thanks for this," I tell him.

"Sure. Where's Roscoe?"

It's exceedingly unusual for me not to have Roscoe at my heels, but I left him with Jules on this occasion. I still haven't told Shay about her, so there's no way I'm going to tell Conor.

"Left him home this time," I say shortly.

Conor nods. "I brought an extra helmet. It's Felicity's, but give it a try."

His girlfriend's helmet is black, thankfully, and fits well enough. We spend the next sixty minutes going over everything in fine detail. Conor is exacting and a control freak, and the lecture makes me antsy. But once I do get on the motorbike, it's fantastic. The feel comes more naturally than I thought it might. I do a series of passes up and down the empty roadway, each time a little faster than the last. The rush intensifies the longer go, I increase my speed and lean into the bike for better aerodynamics as I weave and turn like I'm suddenly Evil Knievel.

I only stop when I finally realize Conor's been shouting and waving his arms at me.

"Get the fuck off my bike," he tells me when I roll up to him.

My heart is beating like a jackhammer. Blood is coursing through me to the point where I can practically feel the flow. Jesus, I can get addicted to anything.

"What's the problem?" I reluctantly swing my leg over the seat and Conor turns off the ignition and sets the kickstand, two things I hadn't thought of.

"You were getting reckless, Danny Boy. Get your own bike if you want to crash it."

"I didn't realize."

"Of course you didn't. *You* wouldn't."

Conor has never liked me. He's always seen nothing but the worst in me. I've given him reason for this, of course, but no matter how much time passes with me on good behavior, it'll never count for him. This is the other reason why I dislike him: he is the embodiment of the voices in my head that say I'm trash and not only will never amount to anything but don't deserve to.

"Give me a fucking break," I say. Even if I agree with his assessment of me, my instinct is to push back. "I was just enjoying the moment. Why can't you ever just let go and do the same?"

Conor's always had a stick up his arse, eternally concerned about his image and controlling things in general. That may have led to his successes, but it's fucking annoying to me—again, probably because I'm the exact opposite. I've never had an ounce of control all my life, starting with the way my parents raised me. Instead of rebelling against that and claiming control over things, I gave in to it. The lack of control, Ms. Patterson tells me, is actually comforting to me because it is what I know best. It's a big part of why I spent so many years seeking out dangerous situations and making poor decisions.

"This isn't about me," Conor says. "You asked for the favor. You need to abide by the conditions that come with it."

"Yeah, yeah," I mumble.

Conor shakes his head and I can tell he's struggling with himself. He feels obligated to help me because of Shay. The best thing that kid ever did was get into a band with these guys. They took care of him when I left home. Shay calls them brothers and though it's a little painful for me to admit, I can see that is what they are to him.

"What have you been up to?" Conor asks.

I appreciate the effort at neutral small talk, even if I can't exactly tell him the truth. "Not a whole lot. Getting anxious for you guys to get back on the road."

Conor smiles the smile that has caused a thousand panties to drop. Though he's committed to Felicity now, he was one of the most sought-after bachelors in the world for a lot of years. Whenever women in my party crowd found out who my brother was, the first thing they asked was whether I could hook them up with the gorgeous guitarist of the Rogue. Conor's always been partial to models and actresses, though, so even if I had some pull there would be no way he'd be up for one of my party girls.

"We're enjoying the break," he says. "We won't even think about recording until next year. The tour wouldn't happen until springtime at the earliest."

It's nearing August now, so this isn't good news for my idle mind. The idle mind that Jules has been filling with things that have me slipping and sliding toward the wrong direction.

"Let me ask you something," I blurt out, unable to withhold speaking my thoughts out loud. "How do you know exactly when you've made the wrong bet on someone?" It's a question I probably should have saved for Ms. Patterson, but it's out there now.

Conor raises his eyebrows as he looks at me. It's clear he's thinking he always knew *I* was the wrong bet. But he gives the question some thought.

"I'm not sure I can define it. But I do know that it's usually realized too late," he says. "If you want to know the truth, it's those times where I've lost the control you seem to think I'm too fond of."

"Like when you slept with Sophie?" I ask without thinking.

Conor's expression hardens. It's not a subject anyone speaks openly about, even though it's well known within the band—and by me because I got the dirt out of Shay. Conor slept with Sophie when Gavin was checked out at the height of his cocaine addiction. It was a spectacular betrayal since Conor and Gavin had been the best friends since age seven. The other huge part of the drama was that it was clear that Conor did it not out of some uncontrolled desire to get laid, but because he was in love with Sophie and probably had been for a long, long time. He had his choice of any woman he wanted and yet he still fell for the one he couldn't have. Despite all that, the three of them somehow put it behind them and moved on.

"Yes," he finally says, "that was a mistake."

"Do you really believe that? I mean, you had to have gotten something out of it. Besides getting off, I mean."

"For fuck's sake," Conor says with a groan. He does not want to talk about this.

"I'm just trying to figure out whether if you do something you pretty much know is a mistake, is it okay because you will still get something worthwhile out of it in the end."

He watches me for a long moment, but I can't see his eyes behind the shades.

"Julia O'Flaherty," he says. "You're seeing her, aren't you?"

I didn't expect that deduction. But fucking Quinn is no fool. Gavin must have mentioned my visit a while back and now Conor's put it together.

"Em, well, just casually," I lie.

"Fuck me," Conor says softly and looks away. "Listen, I never had a problem with her personally. But you'd do well to take Gavin's advice."

"You know what he told me, then?"

Conor looks at me and nods. "Watch your back."

"I am. I will. But there's something I need to sort out with this. Can you please do me the favor of not mentioning this to anyone? I'm asking sincerely. Let me sort it."

I've asked this man for things before. I've begged for his favor and he's granted it only for me to fuck him over. I know he's not inclined to help me again. But I must have gotten through to him on some level—maybe because of that stuff about Sophie, even—because he gives me the answer I want. And it makes me think I might need to give him more credit for the chances he's given me.

"Okay, I'll do that," he says. Then the control freak in him returns and he says, "But if this negatively impacts at all on the band, or on Gavin and Sophie, you better believe I'll step in and shut it the fuck down."

23

When I tell Ms. Patterson I'm thinking of getting a motorbike, her response surprises me. It isn't concern that the things can be dangerous, and I might get hurt, or that I should think about the fact that I might want it for that very thrill.

Instead, she asks, "Where would you have Roscoe if you got a motorbike?"

I have no answer. My poor buddy. I hadn't thought about him with this idea.

"Fuck. I'll have to get one of those ridiculous sidecar things, won't I?" I ask with a laugh. "Maybe get him some doggy goggles. Won't we be a sight?"

Ms. Patterson laughs.

She's in a particularly warm mood today. The last few weeks as I've gotten in deep with Jules have put us off track. Our sessions haven't been productive as I've spent the time trying to avoid talk of my so-called relationship. I don't reward her with any other meaningful talk, either. The good efforts we had been making before Jules came along have stalled.

After diligently trying to break through to me during those fruitless sessions, Ms. Patterson seems to have decided to take a more passive approach today. Her appearance reflects this. She's wearing a floral-patterned dress with suede high-heeled boots that reach her knees. Her hair is down but partially pinned back. She looks lovely and I tell her so.

"Thank you, Daniel, but—"

"Yeah, yeah. I know I'm not to compliment you."

She nods and raises her pen over her notepad as if to signal that we should get down to business.

"Another theater date with your girlfriends?" I can't help but ask.

After a moment of hesitations, she tells me, "I do have plans later."

"Good for you. I won't follow you this time."

"It's funny you say that. I—" she cuts herself off.

"What is it?" I lean forward.

"Nothing." She shakes her head dismissively.

"Now, Ms. Patterson, you know me better than that." I give her a meaningful look. "I don't give up that easily."

The inner struggle she has shows itself on her face. Finally, she says, "I was going to say something to the effect of you following me that way seemed more true to yourself than the way you've been in the last few weeks."

This strikes me as one of those moments where she's dropped her professional distance. It's always those moments that have the most impact. The last time she did that, she told me I had lost my identity. If she was right about that, then does that mean I've attached myself to Jules in place of trying to know myself? And in the process, have I become someone not even Ms. Patterson recognizes? I'm still not in the mood to analyze myself or my recent actions, though. So, as it is one of my favorite things to do with Ms. Patterson, I deflect.

"Well, I'll just have to find a way to fuck up again, then, won't I?" I ask with a laugh. "Maybe don't hurry too fast from the office later? Try not to give me the quick slip, yeah?"

Again with the head shake. But she hasn't lost that warmth. I wonder what it would be like to know her outside of this space. It feels like we could be friends. I obviously amuse her. And I adore her.

Wait, I *adore* her? Is that what I feel for her?

I know I respect her: she's smart.

I also appreciate her: she's loyal; she's never given up on me; she sees the best in me; she believes in me.

I admire her: she's got her life together with friends and a social life that very likely does not include lines of cocaine.

I'm definitely attracted to her: she's a beautiful woman, with what I like to imagine are hidden depths of sexuality waiting to be uncovered. By *me*.

Above all that: I trust her.

I can't apply many of those things to Jules.

The discrepancy between my feelings for the two women is stark. Especially given that it makes me realize I'm sleeping with the wrong one.

———

Not that I have the option of being with Ms. Patterson. I know that. I may lack impulse control and make poor decisions, but I'm aware enough to know my therapist is not a dating option. But does that mean forever?

"If we stopped doing the client-therapist thing," I say, "would there ever be a time we could have contact? Or is all that null and void because of this stuff?" I've basically just spewed my thoughts out loud, but she's used to that sort of thing.

"Null and void," she says firmly, automatically. It feels cold, like the moment when a fire finally dies out.

My disappointment must be visible because she smiles and humors me by saying, "Besides, you wouldn't want to date someone who knows this much about you, would you?"

I don't see it in that context. I just see all the ways she makes me feel good, despite knowing all my bullshit.

"Or to put it another way," she continues, "you've said you don't like it when Jules tries to 'figure you out' as far as why you started heroin. Your upbringing has left you with difficulties getting close to others, so naturally you don't want to expose your deepest hurts at the very start of a relationship."

"See, we'd never have to go through that. Already past it." I grin triumphantly.

"Oh, I'd never stop pointing out how you were manifesting your issues, Daniel," she says with a small laugh. "You'd very quickly tire of me, just—"

Again, she stops herself and I can just about fill in what she would have said: Just like the rest of them. As if she's had a series of relationships gone bad because she couldn't keep from diagnosing her partners. Poor sods.

"Something I'd have to live with," I say with a wink. I want her to know I'm breezing by her inadvertent admission. It would kill her for me to point out I knew exactly what she was saying, and I don't want her to feel exposed like that. I know what that unwanted exposure feels like, after all.

"Hypothetically, anyway." She taps her pen on her notepad. "So, let's talk about how things have gone since I saw you last."

24

"What do you talk about in those therapy sessions, anyway?" Jules is eyeing me from her side of the bathtub we're sharing. It's the big jacuzzi tub in Shay's master bathroom. I rarely go into his bedroom, not since that time I fucked up and made an ass of myself with Jessica. And I've never used the tub. I'm more of a shower guy.

But Jules loves her soaks and has asked several times for us to share one. After our less than successful attempt at a date, I haven't made much of an effort to do things the proper way. We've reverted to the familiar routine I had hoped to avoid for a minute there. It's been all informal hanging out, getting the dogs out for walks or hikes, and going to parties. The constant is plenty of drink and a lack of depth to our conversations. Whereas I understand she's my substitute for heroin, I still don't know what I do for her. She seems content with the fact that I never returned her sentiment of supposedly loving me, which I appreciate.

I got to thinking of that and decided it might be wise of me to give her a little something, and I came up with the tub idea. I went the whole way and set up the room with candles, bubble bath, champagne, and even bloody Sade playing in the background.

Jules was delighted, and I found I don't mind it. The water is warm, and the company is good.

Until she asks about my dear Ms. Patterson.

"Em, just the usual therapy bullshit," I say, trying to evade a real answer. Because that real answer would mean confessing that a good part of the last session we had was about me wanting to see Ms. Patterson in a much more personal way.

She trails her toes over my ribs and asks, "Do you ever talk about me?"

I can't be sure exactly what she's after with this, but I decide to be honest. "Yeah, I told her I'd met you. Told her the very same day, in fact."

"The same day? You had a session planned that day?"

"No. I dropped in on her. I didn't think it could wait."

Jules smiles, and it's obvious she's charmed. But it's for all the wrong reasons.

"I knew that first day you fancied me," she says, "with all that stumbling over yourself to claim you weren't really a Southsider and all."

She's smiling at me and looks so pleased that I don't have the heart to correct her.

"I was rather overwhelmed after our meeting, love," I tell her. I'm eager to move away from this false characterization of how it happened that I told Ms. Patterson about her. And in talking about the day we met, I realize this is an opening to ask her something that's been bothering me for a long time. "Tell me something?"

"What's that?"

"Why'd you kiss me in the park so sudden like?"

Her smile fades a little and when she recovers it, the joy is gone. "You know why," she says softly.

"Tell me."

She shakes her head a little, wary.

"I want to hear you tell me."

With a little shrug, she straightens against the tub and draws her knees to her chest. "I wanted you to know my interest wasn't in *him*."

"Who?" For once, I want her to say his name. Because if she does so in the way I think she will, it will confirm my suspicions about how all this came to be with us—that is, by kissing me, she was only trying to prove a negative.

Now she rolls her eyes. "What are you playing at? I thought we were having a romantic moment here?"

Maybe I should stop. But that's not who I am. "You're saying you kissed me because you wanted to show you weren't interested in *who?*"

She sighs and drops her hands abruptly, splashing water and bubbles up. "Gavin. You know, the fella you were imagining I had some kind of crazy plan to get to through you?" she says with exasperation.

So, there it is. Just what I knew she'd say. She kissed me to distract me from thinking that she was after my connection to McManus. Only, she didn't realize the spark it would ignite. She didn't expect how massive our attraction and our need to escape in each other would be. Should I just count myself lucky that it worked out that way? That even if we're just doing this co-dependent thing with each other, it's better than being alone?

"Do you have regrets, Danny Boy?" she asks.

The question gets to the heart of my internal debate. It's a wake-up call as I realize I don't need to get stuck in my own head any longer. It's time to just let this thing be whatever it's gonna be.

"No, love," I tell her. "If there's one thing about me, it's that I don't do regrets."

"That simple, huh?"

"Has to be. Why? Do you regret kissing me in the park?"

She makes a show of thinking about it just to annoy me, but I keep my patience.

"No, I don't. I just wish it wasn't so hard to convince you that I like you. Or, I guess I should say, I wish it wasn't so hard for you to believe I *could* like you."

She hasn't been shy about telling me she's into me. I haven't returned the favor much. Being naked in this tub with her seems like the perfect place to be more intimate with her—in terms of sharing things, that is. I can, and do, have sex with her wherever I want, so it isn't about that. I decide to take a gamble and finally answer the question she posed during our date.

"You still wanna know about me and heroin?"

"Where is this coming from?" she asks, but I ignore her.

"My parents are a rare breed of fucked-up. They drink a bit much like a lot of others, but that's not really the source of it. It's the fact that they have the inability to understand that their duty is to actually take care of their kids. They were so fucking checked out, that it was up to me to raise myself as soon as I could figure things out—which I had to do quick. And then even more so when Shay was born. I was the one that raised that kid. Day in and day out, I was the one who made sure he had meals, and brushed his teeth, did his schoolwork, and everything in between. Our loser parents had no interest in us."

I get lost for a moment thinking of the incredible loneliness I felt. It was the strongest emotion of my childhood, with anger being a close second. The two were a volatile mix and led to me acting out in class as a way to release my bottled-up resentment.

"Anyway, I first did heroin out of exhaustion. I was so fucking tired of being the one to get Shay through the day. My whole life had been consumed with making sure he was okay. I needed a break. Some kind of reprieve, you know? But I couldn't fathom purposely stepping away. And so, when I saw the state heroin got some of my mates into—you know, that detached bliss—I thought, this is the temporary fix for what ails me. I'll just take a taste. Just to see what it's like, for once, to not have any worries."

I feel my body go slack as I think of that first hit. It was an all-consuming sensation of relaxation. I had no cares in the world.

"I might have been able to walk away after the one time, even as addicting as that shit is," I continue. "But in the back of my mind, I didn't want to. I *wanted* to become an addict. Because that would give me the excuse to drift away from all the responsibilities I felt for raising Shay. It would give me an out from the near constant negativity in my head. Rather than keep fighting the certainty that I was worthless, I just proved all that right. I decided I wasn't worth the effort. At eighteen, I was done with the struggle. Shay was thirteen when I left him for the smack. *That's* the kind of guy you're with."

Jules is quiet for a moment, but she does reach out and pulls one of my hands into hers. Our fingers are wrinkled with too much time in the water.

"Shay managed, didn't he?" she asks softly.

"Spectacularly well," I agree. "So, me not being there was probably the best thing."

"That's not being fair to yourself."

I stare at the candle on the corner of the tub. Melted wax is pooling and threatening to spill over the top. I'm transfixed by the slight flicker of the flame. Finally, I shrug.

"Turned out I was very good at heroin," I say with a smile. "I could handle it pretty damn well. And I even sorted out my own detox method."

"You miss it." It's a statement. Not a question.

"Oh, fuck yeah." I laugh without humor.

"Well, you do make it sound good."

I stare into her eyes and find she's giving me a concerted neutral look. But I can't help but read into what she said. I feel certain she would get straight out of this tub and go out onto the streets with me to find and try H as long as we did it together.

Maybe I had it all wrong about her being dangerous because of some thing she still had for McManus. And maybe I had it all right about her wanting me in order to ease her into heroin. What I know for certain is that she's even more lost than I am.

This is the kind of temptation—enabling, really—I should run from. Instead, I pull her to me and she wraps her legs around my hips and I hold her tight.

And I know *this* is why I haven't told Shay about her. Because being with her is a half-step toward slipping back into my old ways. I tell myself that I *won't* let myself fall, that I'm purposely playing close to the line simply for the thrill of it.

But I have no reason to believe myself.

25

I'm home on a late Saturday afternoon, lounging in the Man Cave with Roscoe when Shay calls. I mute the football game I'd been watching and answer.

"Hey, kid. What's the craic?"

"I was calling to ask you the same," he replies. "It's been a while."

It has. I've purposely "missed" Shay's calls in the last month, avoiding him rather than lie to him about Jules. I still don't know what it is I have going on with her, what I need from her. And so, I've decided not to share with my brother that I've been spending time with her. What good would it do? It'd only make the kid worry all the more about me. He's got enough on his plate, what with Marty running around at gay bars in San Francisco and stirring up the gossip headlines once more. Jesus, that guy has really broken free of the old marriage bonds in the most spectacular fashion.

"Figured you've been busy. Your man Marty has really upped his game," I say.

Shay laughs and it's exactly what I love to hear from him. If I gave it much thought, I'd probably realize that part of my instinct to say random things for effect started long ago when I would try so hard to make my kid brother laugh just to brighten the darkness of our childhood.

"What's been going on in your world?" he asks.

"Ah, not much to report. Roscoe and I just do our thing, you know?"

"Good. That means you'll be free to join us in Los Angeles."

"Los Angeles?" I immediately think of whether Shay will spring for a private plane to get me out there so that Roscoe can travel easier than if we go commercial.

"Yeah, Gavin's got a grand plan to get the band together there. He and Sophie have rented a house and we'll all stay for a week. Sort of a thing to get us all on the same page since Marty's got some issues he's working out."

"Ah, isn't that sweet of him," I say. "He's such a touchy-feely fucker." I never hesitate to take the piss out of any of those guys and they give it right back.

"It's probably Sophie's doing more than anything, but it's not a bad idea."

"When is this thing?"

"Em, August something." He goes quiet for a second, probably looking at the calendar app on his phone. Returning, he says, "About ten days from now, in fact."

Shite. That coincides with the trip Jules and I have committed to. That day we spent looking at destinations all over the world led us to reject Europe as we've both traveled it extensively. America didn't thrill us. We moved southward in our research and settled on Tulum, a beach town on the Caribbean coastline of Mexico's Yucatán Peninsula. We've booked a flight and a hotel right on the white sand. In the spur of the moment, it seemed like a fantastic idea. As the days have passed, though, I've thought less fondly of it. Jules and I are a combustible mix. Also, I'm not happy about the fact that we'll have to board our dogs. It'll be the first time I'm away from Roscoe since he found me.

And now I have to come up with some sort of excuse to tell my brother. I don't like doing this. It's a step backward and another red flag that what I'm doing by being with Jules isn't right. I should just come clean and tell him about her. But I still can't bring myself to do that.

Instead, I go off on how Ms. Patterson has me working a special program at that very time, one where I'm doing daily in-person check-ins with her and other lies to back it up. It's remarkable even to me how easily it all flows. In the past, I wouldn't have thought twice about concocting a story like that to suit my needs. Now, it gives me a sick feeling in my stomach. Still, I stick with it.

"It's probably for the best anyway," I say. "You guys need time together—for your intervention with Marty, right? To let him know it's okay to come out as a gay man?"

"He'll not be doing that," Shay says wearily.

The stress in Shay's voice isn't over worrying that Martin is gay. It's that his friend is clearly struggling and if one of those Rogue fellas is struggling, they all struggle. Shay doesn't like when there is tension or drama within the band. Rogue has been the main focus of his life. It gave him a purpose when he could have just as easily followed my lead. In fact, I tried many times to get him lost in heroin with me, starting when the kid really was still a kid (remember—I ain't no saint). And it was McManus who made sure it didn't happen. Shay's had fierce loyalty to that guy ever since. The band gave him stability. It gave him a *life*. It's no wonder he lives and dies by what's happening within it.

"All this tabloid shite will fade away, kid," I tell him. "It always does. And then you lads will get on with it, won't you?"

Shay is quiet for a moment. Then I hear him take in a deep breath and exhale. Not too long ago, he could have been enjoying a ciggie, but he quit recently, and it seems to be for good this time.

"Yeah, sure. It'll be grand," he says. "Anyway, I'll miss having you there in Los Angeles. But I'm glad you're really committing to this therapy stuff. It gives me peace, you know?"

I close my eyes tightly, feeling a burn in my chest. "Yeah, I know it does, Shay."

26

The words aren't coming, and I'm once more fixating on the awful paint color covering Ms. Patterson's office walls. Who would pick such a shade of green when you're supposed to be relieving people of their burdens anyway?

This is my last session with Ms. Patterson before Jules and I go to Mexico. I've resolved to tell my therapist about the mixed feelings I've been having about Jules. And to also come clean about the fact that I haven't told Shay about Jules.

Instead, I say, "Tell me it wasn't you who picked the paint job here."

Ms. Patterson looks around the space as if seeing it for the first time. "You don't care for it?"

"Jesus, no. It's awful. It's a bloody *reason* to need therapy in itself."

She laughs, and we share a moment of sustained eye contact, each of us amused.

"It was this way when I took over the space," she says. "I was much more interested in changing out the furniture, honestly. I wanted pieces that would be comfortable. Lighting that wasn't harsh."

"Well, that part is all right. But maybe you can change up the paint one of these days? Hell, I'd come in after hours and help you with it."

"That's very kind of you, Daniel." Her appreciation is genuine, but we both know she'd never take me up on such an offer. Our contact is to be limited to our sessions during normal office hours.

"Well, anyway, I'm going to miss both of our sessions next week."

"Why's that?" She feigns disinterest but raises her pen to take notes.

"Jules and I are taking a little holiday. All the way to Mexico."

There's no hiding her reaction this time. She's surprised.

"I didn't realize you were that serious," she says carefully.

"I haven't told you a whole lot, have I?"

"You have been a bit evasive on the details."

I nod. And then I spend most of the hour session telling her everything. Every little and big thing. I tell her how Jules showed up at my house and suggested we were fucked-up and should be together for that reason. I tell her how I went to see Gavin and he warned me away from her. I tell her how I disregarded that advice in favor of believing she and I had to try to rise above the low expectations everyone, including us, has of ourselves. I tell her how that hope crashed and burned when our date turned into Jules seeing me only through the lens of heroin. I tell her how Jules has pulled me in subtle and overt ways toward my old life, that we drink too much, and rely on sex as our connection. In conclusion, I tell her that I believe Jules would sink with me into a heroin oblivion if I so much as nod in that direction, and that being with her is like a test I desperately need to pass but haven't done the proper studying for.

The silence that fills the room after this is excruciating. I open my mouth to demand some kind of response, but she holds up a finger and stops me. I watch as she gets up from her chair and goes to the door of the waiting room. She closes it behind herself and is gone for three or four minutes before returning.

"Okay, the best I could do was get us another ten minutes," she says.

Glancing at the time on my phone, I realize I spoke non-stop until just past what was supposed to be our end point. Ms. Patterson must have another client lined up. But she's convinced that person to come in late. For me. That effort makes me happier than I know it should. She's only doing her job. But it somehow feels like more.

"First, I have to say I'm pleased with the thought you've applied to all this."

Once more, I open my mouth to speak and she shuts me down with a finger in the air.

"That doesn't mean I'm going to praise you for your decision-making. You may have been able to recognize a lot of self-destructive tendencies and decisions, but you haven't steered away from them the way I would hope."

"I'm only human." I give her my best sheepish grin.

She doesn't fall for my attempt to lighten the mood. "You're playing a dangerous game, Daniel. You've already said you recognize that."

"Ay, it's true."

"Tell me, what is the best-case scenario with being with Jules?"

"What do you mean?"

"I'm asking what, in your mind, do you hope to gain out of this relationship?"

I struggle to answer, and she uses the opening to lay bare everything bad about being with Jules.

"This relationship consists of sex, drug temptations, a disregard for the support you need in your recovery—and has to be *hidden* from your brother. Tell me what is the good that comes out of this?"

"Well fuck me," I say with a laugh. "Put it like that and I've got no answer, have I?"

"We've talked about your reflex to make a joke of things. Let's put that aside at this moment. Time is running short. Soon, you'll be off to Mexico with the woman you've described as a threat to your sobriety."

"Ah, you know I've never blamed anyone but myself for my problems. If I slip up, I won't put that on Jules. Every fucking thing in my world is a temptation. So, this is on me, no matter what."

"Of course, it is. But why set yourself up for a harder time? Why willfully keep Jules so close to you when it only exacerbates the possibility you'll make the wrong choice and use again?"

I shake my head. "I dunno. Maybe because the sex is so damn good?"

Ms. Patterson straightens in her chair. "Surely she's not your only option for that."

With a wink, I tell her, "Just wanted to see what your reaction might be."

She sighs, frustrated. I don't blame her. I'm being a bastard. I'm wasting the effort she made to grant me more time. See, it's not like I don't know when I'm fucking up at the time that I'm actually fucking up. I just can't help myself. Lack of impulse control, is the official diagnosis. It's either that, or like I said, I'm a bastard.

Getting back to the point, Ms. Patterson says, "You said Jules is a substitute addiction, one that isn't as dangerous as the real thing. But what happens when whatever she gives you isn't enough anymore?"

This puts it all in perspective. I can see now more than ever what my draw to Jules is. She's my way of testing myself. My way of seeing whether I really have shed my old identity or if I'll go crawling back to it. Have I really changed? *Can* people change? That's what I'm trying to sort out. And like Ms. Patterson pointed out, I'm playing a dangerous game in pursuit of the answer. But that's what I do. *That* part of me hasn't changed.

"Ah, my dear Ms. Patterson," I say with glibness I don't really feel, "that's the very thing I'm after finding out, amn't I?"

She takes a deep breath and exhales. "Okay, we'll figure it out together."

That measure of support strikes deep inside my chest. I think my adoration for her has escalated to love.

Standing, she signals that our time is up, and I reluctantly join her.

"You'll take extra care on this trip, won't you?" she asks.

"I'll be back in one piece," I promise.

She hesitates. There's something more she wants to say but can't. Or won't.

I want to reach out and hug her. I want to wrap my arms around her and thank her for caring for me. For being the one true constant in my life. But for once, I do the right thing by restraining myself.

"Adios, señorita."

The smile she gives me is just as conflicted as the hesitation she had a moment ago. But there's nothing I can do about it. Roscoe and I are off.

27

The flights to get to Tulum are long but afford us the opportunity to become double members of the esteemed mile-high club: once on the way from Dublin to our first stop in Atlanta, and again from there on to Cancún. It's obnoxious, I know, but you gotta live a little.

After more than fourteen hours of flying, we're ready to dash right into the crystal blue waters. But first we connect with our private car service for the nearly two-hour drive to Tulum, which finds us chasing the late afternoon daylight. We could have taken a basic taxi or even a shuttle bus, but this is one of the concessions I've made to Jules' desires for the VIP treatment.

I'm footing the bill for this trip since Jules made it clear it was *my* idea to travel. She also made her preferences known for wanting first class airfare along with top of the line hotel and other accommodations for our activities. A part of me wonders if she thinks I've got Gavin McManus-level wealth. I may live in a posh house and drive an expensive car, but neither is mine and I don't have the bank account to back them up.

I've never had a huge attachment to money. It's always been someone else's that I enjoyed, like with my party circuit "friends." Or it was Shay's when he bailed me out on numerous occasions. It wasn't until this last part of Rogue's tour where I was put on salary, that I ever associated money with something that I earned. The cause and effect of me actually doing a job and getting compensated for it resonated for the first time in my life. I became thoughtful about where and how I spent it. And because so much was provided for me first on tour, and then with staying at Shay's, I've built up a good savings. So, I'm happy to pay for the trip, but this isn't going to be a *Lifestyles of the Rich and Famous* episode. We flew business class. And while we're staying at a boutique hotel right on the sand, it's the bargain one that goes for two hundred dollars a night, rather than the ones on either side of us that charge upwards of six hundred dollars a night.

We discover it still affords us our very own piece of paradise when we get checked into our ocean view bungalow.

Jules pulls aside the mosquito netting of the king size bed and falls face first onto it with a happy moan. I join her, though I'm on my back, raised up on my elbows so I can see the water glimmering in the early evening sunlight. There's not one cloud in the sky and all we can hear is the gentle crashing of the waves and the breeze rushing through the willowy palm trees reaching high into the sky.

What I wouldn't give to have Roscoe here. I can just imagine us wandering for hours along the beach, hunting for sticks to throw along the way. Walking next to me in this vision is not Jules, but Ms. Patterson. I indulge in this fantasy for another minute, curious how my brain will fabricate the non-office version of her. Her hair is down, blowing softly about her face. She wears a tropical patterned pink and green mini dress, showing off her lovely legs. There's a smile on her face as she reaches for my hand.

"Let's get a margarita," Jules says as she pulls herself upright. "Then we need to test that water."

I nod, reluctantly letting go of the fantasy that doesn't involve her.

We wander down the beach as the sun disappears. The thick air cools only slightly, but the water feels refreshing, as we let the ebb and flow of the gentle waves wash over our feet. Despite the built-in romance of our surroundings, I don't take Jules' hand and she doesn't seek out mine. I only now realize why Ms. Patterson's first response to learning Jules and I were going on holiday was to be surprised that we were "that serious." Going away together as a couple is on a different level than casually hanging out back in Dublin. It feels awkward between us again, and I suspect we're both eager to get some alcohol into the mix.

Luckily enough, this strip of white sand beach is custom made to offer tourists like ourselves that kind of relief. We happen upon a combination restaurant and mezcal bar and plant ourselves in two padded chairs under a charming web of exposed bulbs which provides a soft glow against the darkening night sky. We're seated on the open-air beach side of the restaurant, but there's an indoor portion which appears to offer live music as we can hear it out here. If a drink or two doesn't loosen the mood, I'll suggest we join the crowd inside.

"Shall we toast?" I ask after we've been given our margaritas.

The request catches her in the midst of taking a gulp and she pulls the glass away from her lips with an impish smile.

"Sure, let's," she says and raises her glass.

"Eh," I say, scrambling to think of something witty and light. We're on holiday, after all. No need to get maudlin. But, of course, that doesn't come through when I open my big gob. "To change. Or at least to finding out if change is even possible."

Jules watches me for a moment before smirking. "Okay, Danny Boy," she says and takes a drink.

My margarita goes down easy within a few swallows and we're both soon on our second round.

"Do you ever think about that, Jules?" I ask. "Do you ever think about whether people can truly change?"

"Not really. I think you are who you are. No use overthinking it."

"That's why I'll always be the heroin addict to you, then?"

She scoffs. "Oh, is that what I think?"

"Seems to me, yeah."

"Well, it's not true."

"Then why is that what it always comes back to with you? *That's* what you asked about after we fucked the first time. *That's* what you asked about on our first date."

This accusation gets her back up. "For fuck's sake, you can't put that on me. *You're* the one who confessed it the second bleeding time we ever talked. And then *you're* the one who brought it up the last time, when we were having a bath."

I finish my drink and think about the fact that she's not wrong. I did bring it up those times. I've obviously been preoccupied with my addiction history, what with all the self-analysis I've been doing.

Jules isn't done having her say, though. She pulls me from my thoughts, telling me, "*You* have made it seem like an important part of your . . . identity."

There's that fucking word again. *Identity*. For a second, I wonder whether Jules spoke with Ms. Patterson and that's why she used it. I have to talk myself down from this paranoia. It has to be paranoia, right? This has to be one of those times when I need to make sure I'm looking at what is *really* happening rather than letting my mind do tricks on me based on the narrative that will best suit my purposes. Which would be what at this moment?

I've been testing her, I realize. By bringing this up on the first night of our holiday, by turning our evening into an argument over how she views me, I've been looking for her to admit she *wants* that old version of me. Because if that's the truth of the matter, then she truly is with me so we can get drug-lost, and knowing that would make it all that much easier for me to give in. To give up on everything I've done to leave that version of me behind.

Jules stands and moves in front of me, forcing me once more to pull away from my thoughts. She's wearing a gauzy white dress over her maroon bikini. The lights overhead shine perfectly for me to see the outline of her body, including the shape of her hips and the swell of her breasts. It's once more incredibly easy to get lost in our sexual

attraction. To be distracted from everything else. To succumb to this
addiction to her body. I pull her hand until she's sitting on my lap.
I'm ready to forget once more what troubles me about her, ready to
turn this into some kind of semi-public sexcapade.

But she surprises me by touching my face with tenderness.
"Danny Boy," she says softly. "You are a boy, aren't you? So ill-
equipped to connect with others. With *me*. You won't ever believe
that I like you because of *you*, not because I'm after Gavin or looking
to do heroin with you."

I laugh uncomfortably and look away. She's right. I am *ill-
equipped*. I don't know how to properly connect with people. I'm
deficient in that way. She turns my face back to hers with her fingers
on my chin.

"It is possible, you know?" she says. "It's both possible that you are
worthy of being liked—*loved*, even—and that I don't have any bad
intentions."

Meeting her eyes, I will myself to believe her. Because I want to
believe her. I want to believe this can all be real. That I can be something else. That I can matter to someone. And so I force myself to
dismiss all my doubts. We're on vacation anyway, aren't we? This is
as good of a time as any to play with the fantasy that sees me finding
some kind of normalcy.

28

The next several days pass in a blur of the best escapism I've ever known outside of heroin. The crystal-clear ocean water is eighty degrees, the sun heats the days to near ninety degrees, and we indulge in a constant low-level buzz from beers and tequila. We spend a ton of time napping on the beach during the days, and we spend our nights touring the various bars on the sand before falling into bed back at the hotel. We don't sleep for long periods, as one of us wakes in the night and initiates sex—hence the need for naps. It's comfortable and easy, even if it also feels surface-level to me. We get along, sure, but that connection still feels elusive, no matter how hard I try to force it. On the other hand, to any outside observer, we very well could be on our honeymoon.

We aren't complete heathens, though, as we do make time to explore beyond our hotel beach, including a trip to a *cenote*, or underwater sinkhole and cave. The water here is pure, especially with the focused sunlight shining down from the cave opening overhead. We snorkel, float on our backs, and climb the side of the rockface to do a little cliff diving.

Another excursion we seek out is a guided tour through the Sian Ka'an reserve, which finds us in our own small boat gliding through mangrove-lined canals of crystalline waters, slowing down to view the wild birds we encounter like storks, herons, osprey and vultures. Part of the way through the day, our guide fits us with life jackets and has us jump into the water. We are not only refreshed but thrilled by the way the current gently but firmly pulls us along the same route the Mayans had used a thousand years before.

Jules even convinces me to try sunrise yoga right on the white sand one day since Tulum is well known for its "healing energy." I spend most of the time alternating between watching the sky change from pink to purple to burnt orange, to watching Jules contort in ways I never knew she could. It gives me ideas for things we can try later.

The last planned part of our trip is a visit to the local well-preserved Mayan ruins. The area once contained trading operations for turquoise and jade and were fortified by a thick, three-sided wall as protection. These cliffside limestone structures overlooking the ocean are incredible, but I'm even more taken by the iguanas lounging unafraid of us tourists tramping through their space. I seriously consider trying to scoop one up to take back to our hotel to have as a buddy while we're here.

"Yes, I miss my dog, too," Jules says with a wry smile and pulls me away.

There's no shade in this area and by the time we're done with the sightseeing, sweat is dripping down the backs of our necks. We have a long, hot walk back to the car park before we can find relief and decide to go for a dip in the ocean before that.

But the winds are whipping the water into wild waves and so it isn't advised that we climb down the hill from the ruins to cool off. There are some kite surfers taking advantage of the weather, and their spectacular tricks make me want to join them. Not that I know how to kite surf, but what I wouldn't give for that kind of adrenaline rush. It reminds me of Shay's newest hobby. He's hooked up with some lads in San Francisco who are teaching him how to sail and apparently, they can get moving fast enough to get your heart racing. He and I have that need for a thrill in common. Well, his is fixated on the actual act of being in a dangerous situation like car racing or high-speed sailing, even as he ultimately is the one in control. Mine is more the danger of giving up all control, like with heroin or making thoughtless decisions like climbing thirty feet up a lighting rig ladder to get a closer view of Rogue playing live. I managed to come out relatively unscathed with the first bit, but I did damage with that second one. I lost my grip and crash-landed right onto Shay, breaking his wrist. Conor, Mr. Perfect, took it personally and came to Shay's aid. He sucker-punched me and sent me to my arse. It was a whole thing. But for a brief moment it was a fucking rush and made it all worthwhile, though I'm sure Shay and his mates thought otherwise.

It's with all of this in mind that I take a step closer to the edge of the cliff, drawn to the idea that I could jump in from here. I think of what we learned back up at the ruins, about the figure with a bird's wings and tail that had been chiseled above the doorway of the Temple of the Frescoes. It's known as the diving god and thought to represent a Mayan deity who protected the people. Might his spirit still be here today? I imagine the instant relief from the heat I'd feel if I were to sink deep into the water below. I ignore the fact that the waves would surely batter me against the rocks as helplessly as a ragdoll. Or, maybe that's the real draw of it, the absolute lack of control—assuming that diving god never appears and my leap leads to my demise.

I feel a hand on my shoulder and I pull against it, ready to take the jump.

"Danny Boy," Jules says insistently. "What are you doing?"

Blinking, I take a deep breath and let her pull me back a few steps.

"You were getting too close to the edge. You know that?"

"I, em, I dunno."

She watches me curiously, but I look back at the ocean. That wind is blowing in dark clouds. Looks like we'll be able to cool off one way or the other soon enough.

29

The rain comes during the short drive back to the hotel. It's still warm and humid out, so the downpour isn't really a bother. We stand out in it in front of our bungalow, letting the fat drops of water soak us through before jumping in the ocean for a swim. Standing waist-deep, we watch, mesmerized, as the rain pelts the surface of the water. Pulling on the goggles we'd grabbed from our snorkel kits, we dive under the water and look up at the rain from the opposite angle. Even with the sun muffled by clouds, it's still bright enough that the water retains its soothing turquoise shade. The raindrops create a vast, shimmering blanket that ripples along the surface. The scores of drops somehow work in concert to create a soothing, tapping rhythm.

It's a magical experience.

We come up for air and lock eyes, giddy smiles on our faces.

This is the moment I feel something change. I finally feel like I can relax, that I can trust her. Our idyllic surroundings reinforce this sense of ease, I'm sure. But we've also spent the last five days enjoying each other. In the end, all I really needed was to give it a chance. A *real* chance.

I pull her to me and kiss her. Our goggles crash and we laugh before peeling them off. When I take her mouth in mine, I give her something I've held back all this time. I give her tenderness. I want to be good to her. I want to care for her. I want a genuine connection. She must feel something's different because she breaks the kiss to look at me. Then she wraps her arms around my neck and buries her face into my chest.

The rain coming down around us intensifies and the sound of it crashing against the ocean is loud. Still, I hear her when she tells me, "I love you."

Without a word, I take her hand and we make our way back to the bungalow.

We have an outdoor shower that's partially surrounded by a bamboo fence and I pull her into it. We tug off our suits while kissing. Instead of the rough, impatient kisses borne out of the animalistic attraction we've always known, we now trade deep, slow, searching kisses. I stop and hold her face in my hands just so I can look at her. She's panting slightly, her mouth open and hungry. Water from the shower and the rain that's still coming down cascades over her naked body. Her breasts rise and fall as she watches me take her in. She's gorgeous, every bit of her—from her expectant blue eyes, to the delicate dimple at her chin, to her firm tits, to the slight, womanly swell of her belly, to the trimmed hair between her legs. I want every part of her and drop to my knees. She tastes like the salty ocean. I tease my tongue all over her before focusing on her clit and soon her body is shaking against me.

Jules wraps her arms tight around me when I move up, needing a second to recover. It makes me smile. And then I tell her something I will end up regretting.

"I fucking love you, Jules."

She moans in response. It's a happy, satisfied sound, but I intend to change the nature of it to something else. Grabbing her hand, I take her inside. We're both naked and wet and I use a towel to gently dry her body, from her hair down to her toes. I give myself a once over and then pull Jules to the bed and into my arms for another one of those tender kisses.

When she reaches for my cock, I pull her hand away. I want this to go slow. She's already had one orgasm and there's time for more. I'll delay my own gratification along the way. I trail my hands over her skin, exploring her body in a way I've never done before. Our fierce attraction has always meant we were concerned with getting off rather than connecting. That's all well and good, and I'm not turning into some sort of new age tantric sex guy, but there's nothing wrong in this version. Not when it builds up the anticipation.

I replace my hands with my mouth, drawing my tongue and lips and teeth over her shoulders and breasts and nipples, before moving downward. Her sensitive body jumps when my mouth touches the skin behind her knee and then her inner thighs.

"Danny," she breathes shakily.

It doesn't seem like she can take much more, but I turn her on her belly and run my hands from her shoulders down her back and over her tight ass, squeezing there and barely able to stop from doing more. But I persist, again replacing my hands with my mouth even as my cock drips from the desire I'm trying to hold back. I wet my fingers with it to use as lubrication, though I find Jules doesn't need any help. Spreading her legs with one hand, I use the other to explore her and she pushes against me, encouraging me so that I use another finger and go deeper.

"I need you," she says, her hands reaching back for me, trying to direct me.

I turn her on her back once more and move between her legs, pushing myself slowly, deeply, into her and watching her reaction. Her eyes are half closed and her half smile is pure bliss. When she locks her legs around my hips and I feel her tighten up around me, I know exactly how that bliss feels. She grabs my biceps, holding tight as I lean down to kiss her. Testing my strokes and positioning, I find the right spot to get her writhing against me for her second orgasm. It makes her turn her head away from my kiss so she can cry out before dissolving into a happy, laughing moan.

"Come for me now," she says, grabbing my backside and pulling me deep into her.

Before long, I've done as she asks and collapse on top of her with my own smile.

It's the first time I've ever made love in my life.

————

"You have lovely hands," Jules says as she holds one of mine in hers.

We're lying on our backs on the bed, naked and lazy as the rain continues to come down and create its pitter-patter music against the roof of our bungalow.

I wonder if she can see the old needle marks in between my fingers, but I don't ask. I've been doing a good job of not thinking about heroin since after that first night of this trip. On any other regular day, it comes to mind frequently. But this has been a true escape.

"They do the job," I say with a laugh.

"Very well, indeed." She turns on her side and snuggles into me.

"Jules, you know what I'd love?"

"Hmm?"

"For you to sing for me."

"Really?"

"I've heard your recordings, but it'd be fantastic to hear you live."

She looks up at me and smiles. "What would you have me sing?"

"Anything you like, love. Surprise me."

"I'll have to think about that. I'd want it to be just right, you know, to be able to warm up my voice some."

It charms me that she'd want to put special effort into it. I would have been happy for her to sing me a little tune right here and now.

"You ever think you'd take another shot at it?" As much as she tried to convince me her artsy side gig of painting women pays the bills, it's obvious that she just gets by. So, if her real talent is singing, it seems logical that she'd pursue that once more.

"Oh, I don't know. I think about it sometimes. It's just . . ."

"Just what?"

"I'd need a helping hand back in. By someone who has some power in the industry."

I think about that for a long moment. And then I say something else I'll come to regret. "Maybe I can talk to Shay about it."

"Really? That'd be fantastic," she says excitedly.

I go tense and she must feel it because she quickly tries to scale back her reaction.

"I mean, if one day I wanted to explore that. I'm not there right now. I'm really happy with what I'm doing with the painting."

I let it go, preferring to go along with her revised framing rather than question it. Because questioning it would mean I'd have to start back to doubting her intentions all over again. I just want to linger in this good connection we've found today.

30

It's early evening by the time we finally shower and dress. The rain is still coming down and expected to last through most of the night, which is too bad since we're leaving tomorrow. Neither one of us feels like going to one of our local bars for the night, but Jules volunteers to run out to get us dinner since our hotel doesn't have room service.

There's no television in our room and an internet signal is spotty at best. This hasn't been a problem as our nights up until now have been spent out, with plenty of drink to occupy us. I pace restlessly as I wait for Jules to come back. That feeling of calm I had earlier has disappeared, replaced by trepidation. I worry I've set something in motion with declaring my love for Jules. I've never done that before. Well, not with that kind of genuine feeling. I've definitely told women I love them, but it always had some sort of angle behind it, usually in pursuit of securing the next high.

I don't know what is supposed to come next. What do people do when they've made this grand statement? Is it supposed to change everything? I just don't fucking know.

My phone buzzes and I'm glad for the distraction. It's Shay, texting me.

"Sorry it's so late," he starts.

It is late in Dublin. Not here. But Shay doesn't know that because I've lied to him. I've lied about all of this stuff with Jules and that reminder ratchets up my unease.

"No worries," I tell him, quickly calculating that it'd be about midnight in Dublin. "Not that late."

"Everything good?"

"Yeah, sure. It's been quiet. You know, the usual. You?"

"Your special therapy sessions okay?"

Oh fuck. I had forgotten about that story. "Yes, good. Making progress, I think." I close my eyes, wincing over this bullshit. "How's L.A.?"

"Sunny."

Typical Shay. He's not the most verbose fella.

"Marty staying out of trouble?"

"You haven't seen the tabloids? He's got a fresh scandal."

I haven't heard or seen anything about that guy because I've been in this protected bubble. It's been all Jules, the beach, and tequila.

"Oh, that thing," I say, hoping it will suffice. "Par for the course, these days."

There's a long period while I wait for Shay's response. He must know I'm off, and probably suspects I'm using or something. That's how his mind works. He jumps to that conclusion at the slightest indication of me slipping. Of course, I've given him good reason for that over the years.

"I need to ask a favor."

The abrupt change in direction surprises me. My brother is not one to ask for my help.

"Sure. What is it?"

"Marty will be back in town after this trip. Can you check in on him? Be sure he's himself?"

I laugh out loud. The idea that I'm trusted to check up on someone else is foreign. *Am* I capable of that? Have I earned that in Shay's eyes? I feel buoyed at the thought that Shay trusts me to look after his mate.

"Yes, of course," I type, grinning.

"Appreciate it."

And with that, Shay tells me to say hi to Roscoe and signs off.

Fuck me, it feels good to think I've come far enough that my brother can rely on me for this. Mind, it's not a lot of responsibility, but it's *something*. Especially if it's to do with one of his band mate brothers. Shay must really be worried about the state Marty's in. That fella's clearly taking the mid-life crisis plunge and got Shay anxious over it. I resolve to fix things right up if I find Marty in a self-destructive way.

I'm so hyped on the idea that I forget my usual reticence where Rogue is concerned and tell Jules all about it when she returns, loaded down with bags and dampened all over again by the rain.

"You're his minder, are you?" she asks, bemused.

"Well, I'll do what I can."

She nods without conviction but goes on to tell me she had internet connection at the restaurant and got caught up on the latest goings on with our man Marty. Seems he hooked up with Lainey Keeler, one of the most famous actresses of the day. The press has jumped on it and is being especially hard on Lainey, calling her the homewrecker of Martin's marriage.

"Jesus," I say with a sigh. "Those guys have a special talent for airing their dirty laundry."

Perhaps she plays off my new openness to talk about the guys, because she says with forced casualness, "I also found out that Sophie is pregnant again."

"How'd you learn that?" I blurt it out, unable to stop the sudden suspicion that she once more knows too much.

"Gavin rang and told me," she deadpans, and I believe it for a moment. Then she sighs. "Tabloids again, Danny Boy. He was on some chat show with James Corden and let it 'slip,' though I'm bloody sure that it was well planned out."

"What does that mean?"

"Gavin has always been a calculating bastard. He knows how to play things in the media. So I'm sure this was for a purpose. Maybe to throw the attention his way instead of Marty's for a spell."

"Well, if that's the case, it was good of him, wasn't it?"

She considers this for a moment. Nodding slowly, she says, "I suppose so. Shall we eat?"

31

Jules has brought back plenty of alcohol to go with our fish tacos. We have a six-pack of Negra Modelo, a bottle of Siembra Metl Cenizo mezcal, and a bottle of Siete Leguas tequila. She says it's in honor of our last night, but what we do is get fucking trashed. It starts as a happy kind of drunkenness but takes a turn when she shows me what else she brought back.

"I know you say you don't like it," she tells me quickly when I scowl at the marijuana joints she has in her palm. "But maybe you just need to try it again, without heroin in your system to alter it. It would be so nice to mellow out together with this."

"Have you been especially stressed out, Jules?" I ask with feigned concern, which she ignores.

"No, it's not that. It's just—it's a harmless good time.

She called cocaine harmless as well, but I won't register that until later. Right now, I'm just pissed off that she's pushing this again.

"You go ahead," I tell her. "I'm not into it."

"Just try a little. If it gives you the same bad vibe you had before, then that's it. We'll both stop."

"Jules—"

"Come on, don't be so rigid. I mean, I like you *rigid*, but not about this," she says with a wink.

Her effort to flirt underwhelms me. "I'll have more of the mezcal and leave it at that."

She deflates in disappointment before throwing everything she's got at me. "Come on, baby. You said you loved me, didn't you?"

She's smiling, trying to spin it into a gentle tease, but it feels like pure manipulation. She knows it wasn't easy for me to get to the point where I could say I love her and now she's using it as some sort of . . . what? *Blackmail?* Is having said that I love her supposed to give her free reign to push me into things I don't want to do? Is that what comes with a real relationship? Jesus, the good times we had this trip and *especially* today now feel like a lie.

"Let's enjoy our last night in lovely little Tulum in style," she continues when I'm silent. "We'll smoke a little, and then we'll probably get hungry enough to eat those chicharrónes I bought."

I eye the grease-stained bag she's referring to. Chicharrónes are bits of deep-fried pig skin. We've seen them offered everywhere but haven't been brave enough to try them yet. Looking back at Jules, she seems relaxed, playful even. And I second-guess my hesitation, questioning whether I'm seeing things as they really are or if I'm creating my own version like Ms. Patterson says I do.

I'm halfway to rationalizing things, ready to slip right down into doing what I shouldn't, when Gavin's warning comes to mind.

She's an opportunist.

But what is her game here?

"Let me have your lighter," she says, ready to push forward regardless of the fact that I haven't officially consented.

"What does getting me high get you?" I've said the quiet part out loud, one of my trademarks.

She freezes and looks at me. But she's silent.

"It must get you something. Gavin said you're only after what suits you. So, what does this do for you?"

I can hear her breathing in the quiet between us. Her whole body had gone tense.

"What are you saying?" she asks stiffly. "You talked to Gavin about me?"

"Well, yeah. Seeing how we had something in common, is all."

This explanation doesn't go over well. She's barely containing her fury as she grabs my lighter from the nightstand and gets started on one of the joints.

"And what, exactly, was this conversation about?" Her voice is cold, clipped.

"It was *harmless*, as you might say. I just thought I'd better let him know about you and me." This isn't exactly how it went, but even I know better than to be completely honest at the moment.

"Why?"

"Because the man signs my fucking paychecks, for one."

"That's crap and you know it."

"Jules, meeting you fucked with my head. I couldn't believe it was all random—"

"Jesus, not this again."

"Especially," I continue, "not with the way you brought him up in so many different ways. I had to get his take on just what the fuck I was getting myself into."

She's pacing and smoking, her mind at work.

"And so, he told you that I'm only out for myself, is that it?" she says with exaggerated patience.

"Basically, yeah." Hearing her repeat it back makes me sorry I said anything. It's a shitty thing to say about someone. But before I can get too lost in that feeling, she exhales a stream of smoke directly at me and I'm reminded of how careless she is of my sobriety. Not just careless, but actively detrimental to it. I wave the smoke away and tell her, "Fucking put that thing out." I realize now that she's done a good number on the joint that it's hashish, the more potent form of marijuana. That shite would have really fucked with me.

With that thought comes the memory of something else Gavin said. I hadn't given it much thought at the time since it came along with a barrage of other things he revealed about Jules. But now I do. He said Jules "fed" him cocaine when he was trying to stop. It clicks then, what she was hoping to do by getting me to start up with her here. In much the same way she did with Gavin, she was looking to prey on my weakness. For fun? For control? Because she's screwed up? In the end, I realize the bottom line is that she's fucked up and wanting to drag me down with her.

"Was Sophie sitting her pretty arse right there during this conversation?" she asks.

This concern about Sophie surprises me. "What? No, she wasn't right there."

"And what else did that poncy Southside bastard say, anyway?"

"It's no matter at this point. I didn't take his advice. I decided I wanted to take a chance on you."

"What advice was this?"

I cringe when I realize I let that slip. There's no way this is going to end well. "Just, you know, that I mightn't want to get with you."

"That's what he said? In those words? That doesn't sound like him. And yes," she says, "I do know how the man talks. I know him better than he ever gave me credit for. He's off writing songs to Sophie, giving *her* credit for being the one and only to ever understand him." She scoffs in disgust. "As if I hadn't picked up the very pieces of him all those years. *I* was the one there, helping him through his darkest days. *Not* her."

This revelation has me taking a physical step back. What I had feared from the start has become reality. She's still mad for Gavin. And that means she almost certainly went after me—maybe not right from the start, but as soon as she learned of my connection to him—in order to inch closer to him. She's been biding her time, but it's all coming out now.

"What. Did. He. Say?" she asks slowly, emphasizing each word with barely controlled fury.

Because I figure it can do no more harm than I've already done, I tell her the truth. "He told me to watch my fucking back."

32

O f course, I'm wrong and this only amplifies our row. Jules is beside herself that I not only spoke to Gavin about her but that he denigrated her to me. I'm furious with how clear it now is that she's desperate to have something with him again. It's not even necessarily that she's wanting to be with the man, but she clearly craves his acknowledgement of her place in his life. She feels cast aside and bemoans the fact that she's put herself in this position of repeatedly supporting him, only for him to always choose Sophie.

We go round and round in circles, completely ignoring how this all got started—her insistence that I get high with her. At one point, she breaks down crying and I'm ready to give in just to make this all stop. But then she manipulates things again.

"You don't love me," she whimpers. "You don't. You wouldn't treat me this way if you did."

That's all I can take. Throwing up my hands, I tell her, "How can I love someone I can't trust? How can I love someone who undermines my efforts to stay clean?"

"I'm just your excuse. You put on me everything you don't want to take responsibility for. Aren't you supposed to be owning your shit? Isn't that what your precious Ms. Patterson is all about?"

I don't like that she's brought up Ms. Patterson and it must be clear as day on my face. It's an opening for her to strike out at me and she takes it.

"Oh, there's something there, isn't there?" she says. She wipes dry the tears that had streaked down her cheeks. Her eyes light up as she senses how she can hurt me. "Is it that you've gone and done the most clichéd thing there is and fallen for your therapist?"

I turn away from her and she laughs in response.

"How pathetic—but wait!"

Looking back at her, I see she's got a furrowed brow and a finger to her lips, pretending deep thought.

"Is it," she starts, "a mammy thing you're after with her since yours was basically non-existent? Or do you want to fuck her?"

"I want *you* to fuck off, how about that?" I tell her.

She claps her hands together excitedly. "I know! It's some twisted combination of the two. She's a mammy substitute that you want to fuck. Am I right, Danny *Boy?*"

"You're sick in the fucking head. I should have listened to Gavin. He had good reason to leave you far behind."

That's her soft spot. Anything to do with Gavin. Her face falls and I know I've done damage. But it doesn't stop me from continuing to go after her.

"Why would he choose *you* over a fucking goddess like Sophie, anyway? She's everything you're not, everything you'll never be. I've *seen* the love between them. You never stood a fucking chance."

Her response surprises me. She rushes me, pushing me so hard that I stumble backwards. And she keeps pushing me until I'm up against the door and our bodies are pressed together. Our eyes meet, and I see fire in hers. It's rage and hurt and devastation. And then it turns to need.

We're both breathing heavily, adrenaline jacked up. The anger between us morphs into lust. I know it's not right. I know this is just like an addiction, but I don't have the will to stop it. She doesn't either.

I lean down to kiss her, and she bites my lip. *Hard.* I pull away quickly, but not before the damage has been done.

Wiping at my mouth with the back of my hand, I see a smear of blood and look at her. Had I read her wrong?

The answer is revealed when she grabs at the front of my shorts. She wants to play rough. I can do that—with limits.

I grab a handful of her hair and pull her head back so she meets my eyes again. The forcefulness thrills her, and she watches me with a small, expectant smile. "Let's do this, Jules. I'm game," I tell her. "But if it goes too far for you, you need to say a safe word."

"What word?"

"Gavin," I say, and she closes her eyes. "You say his fucking name if it's too much."

"That's—"

"That's who you'll be thinking of anyway," I finish for her.

She reaches back and slaps me hard across the face. The sting jars me for a second.

"Whatever else you think of me, don't you dare say my feelings for you aren't real. *You're* the one I want, damn it."

Slapping the shite out of me is a funny way of showing it, I think, but don't say.

Because I don't care.

I don't care about anything anymore.

I just want to fuck her.

33

As soon as I come, I pull away from Jules and get up. She goes limp on the bed, her skin still reddened where my hands grabbed and spanked her. I have my own marks where she dug her nails into me and bit me. It was intense, mixing pain and pleasure. I gave her two orgasms along the way. And my one has completely drained me.

I stumble to the bathroom and into the shower, leaning against the wall as the water falls over me. As I try and fail to focus on the aqua colored wall tiles, I realize I'm still drunk.

Stepping out of the shower, I wrap a towel around my waist and fall to my knees to vomit out all the beer and tequila and mezcal. Along with it come tears of sadness and disappointment. I haven't felt this bad—physically and emotionally—in a long time. The pisser of it is that I knew from the start that I was only looking for trouble by being with Jules. I *knew* it. But I went ahead and did it. Just like all the other times in my life where I willfully made the wrong choice.

Once the dry heaving has left me, I grab the sink and pull myself up. Wiping away the steam from the mirror, I examine my haggard face, my raw lip, the scratches and teeth marks all over my neck and shoulders. She never did use the safe word. This is what I got instead.

I rinse the sick from my mouth, dress and open the bathroom door. Jules is curled up on her side in bed, partially covered by the sheet. Her eyes are closed and she's quiet. Slipping on my flip flops, I grab my phone and money clip and head for the door.

"Where are you going?"

Though I stop, I don't look at her. "I gotta get some air. You go ahead and sleep."

She doesn't say anything, and I step out.

It's almost midnight and there's a bright three-quarter moon hanging in the sky among the now sparse clouds. The rain has slowed to just random spitting forced out by the still raging winds. Edging close to the shoreline, I get lost watching the choppy waves come and go.

What a mess this all is. I don't know what I do from here. Surely the damage we did with our words means this thing—whatever it is—is over. And shouldn't it be? For fuck's sake, she's no good for me. She's still hung up on Gavin. She attacked me in the most heinous way, what with her suggestions about Ms. Patterson. What more do I need to understand about this relationship? It's pure shite.

But then those tender moments come to mind. Like when she insisted I was someone she liked, that I'm capable of being loved.

The contradiction of the two versions of her has me confused about what the reality of the situation is.

I fiddle with my phone before forging ahead and calling Ms. Patterson. It's six in the morning there and her answering service takes my message. I claim it's an emergency and wait to get a call back.

The sand is soft between my fingers as I toy with it. This had been an amazing trip, but now the fight we had will always supersede any of the good memories. I wonder how things would have gone had I joined Shay in Los Angeles instead of coming here with Jules. I suppose all our grievances would have come out in another place and time, is all.

I try to sort out the time difference for L.A., thinking I'll give my kid brother a call soon if I don't hear back from Ms. Patterson. It will be good to hear his voice.

My phone buzzes in my hand and I turn it over quickly to find a Dublin number I don't recognize. It must be Ms. Patterson calling from her personal line since it's too early for her to be at the office. That means I've now got a way to reach her directly. I tuck away that interesting information and answer the call.

"Daniel, are you all right?" she asks straight away.

"Yeah. Well, sort of."

"Where are you? It's very loud."

I look up at the palm trees whipping back and forth in the wind. Though it's wonderful to sit out in the still-warm evening and enjoy the scenery, I know I'd better find a quieter place to speak on the phone.

"Give me a minute," I tell her. "I'll get somewhere more protected."

Walking briskly down the beach, I find the beach bar we had visited on our first night. This time, I step into the indoor portion. The walls are painted in vibrant blues, oranges, and reds. Papel picado, those lace paper flags cut with intricate designs, hang from the ceiling along with the same type of string lighting found outside. There are instruments for a three-piece band set on a small stage, but the musicians must be on a break. Good thing, since there is only one couple besides me in the whole place. The weather is likely keeping everyone away. A sad ballad in Spanish is playing on the speaker system.

"Okay, hear me better?" I ask and seat myself in the booth farthest from the couple.

"Much better. Now, what is going on? You do know the hour here, right?"

"Sorry about that. Couldn't be avoided."

The barman steps out from behind the counter and in doing so reveals he had been standing on something to give him more height than he really has. On level ground, he's the size of an overgrown child.

"Drink?" he asks and gestures as if he's downing a bottle. The thought of drinking alcohol right now makes my stomach flip. "Mineral water," I tell him, and he goes back to his bar where he temporarily regains normal height.

"Please, no more delays," Ms. Patterson tells me. Her impatience shows through her usual professional demeanor. But I don't care about that. I just like hearing her voice. I realize in a rush how much I've missed her.

"Okay, well," I start. I have to stop and take a deep breath. As per usual, I'm not exactly sure what I thought I was doing by coming to her with my "emergency." Nor do I know where to begin.

"Where's Jules? Is she okay?"

"Em, yeah. She's fine. She's in our room. I've stepped away. I had to."

"Did something happen?"

"The truth happened," I say simply. "The truth came out with a vengeance tonight."

"Do explain."

I do just that, telling her everything, including Jules' cruel suggestion that I've fallen for Ms. Patterson as a mother substitute. I admit to my own cruelty in return. Finally, I tell her about how it went from anger to sex.

"Daniel, I need to ask you something. I need you to think carefully and answer as truthfully as you can."

"Okay. Always do."

"Was the sex consensual?"

I laugh. "Yes, it was. I don't need to think about it. She was very much a part of wanting it and making it happen."

"You said you were very upset. When emotions run high, the lines can become blurred—"

"Listen, I made her come *twice*. Does that help? She wanted it the same as I did. *That's* why we're so dangerous together. Because we so readily fuck with each other's heads and bodies."

I hear her take a breath as she absorbs this.

Finally, she says, "Okay, so what is the emergency?"

In the brief seconds between the end of the song playing and a new one starting, I can hear something on the line. It sounds like fabric shifting.

"Are you . . . are you in bed?" I ask.

Ms. Patterson hesitates. "I, em, well, it's just past six in the morning on a Sunday. I haven't quite started my day, Daniel."

I like the visual this conjures. I imagine her hair is sleep-tousled and she's wearing a man's pajama top and only panties below. Her skin is warm, her eyes closed as she rests against the pillow and speaks with me. Then I have another thought.

"Are you alone?"

"That's not your concern. Now, tell me what the emergency is?"

I strain to hear more on our connection as a lively, accordion-heavy song ramps up. I don't think there's anyone with Ms. Patterson. I'm glad to have her to myself.

"It's that thing we always talk about," I tell her. "How I need to separate reality from the way I tend to spin things."

The barman returns with a bottle of mineral water, a glass and a small bowl of lime wedges. I nod my thanks and the little fella wanders away.

"You have concerns over your perception of this fight you had?"

"No, that I see clearly. It's this feeling after. The fact that I *know* it's not fucking good to be with her and yet at the same time I think it's exactly what I deserve."

"Let's explore that," she says.

I slump back in my seat, relief flooding my body. I'm overcome with gratitude for her willingness to stick with me.

We talk and it's an exchange that lasts through the night for me and the morning for her. I'm able to stay put and enjoy several bottles of mineral water since the barman never bothers to kick me out. And Ms. Patterson goes about her day with me on the line. As the time goes by I learn she has a sister who she speaks with every day because she has to put me on hold to take her call. I also learn that she drinks coffee in the morning and tea the rest of the day, and she takes both straight, with no milk. I learn that she's never seen

Rogue play live as she prefers old-school jazz, like the Ella Fitzgerald she plays in the background. I enjoy learning her morning routine, listening to her prepare coffee, heat up something that had come from the freezer, shush her meowing cat as she feeds it, and finally boot up a computer. I imagine her sitting at her kitchen table near a window, light streaming in and warming her through as she puts her feet up on the empty chair opposite her. I'd love to be a part of that picture, maybe on that other chair, her feet on my lap. And Roscoe leaning against my leg as he likes to do, having somehow made peace with the cat.

"You there?" Ms. Patterson asks.

"I am." I clear my throat as a pretext to clearing that fantasy from my head. "Just got lost for a minute. What were we talking about?"

"That Jules has become a way for you to grant legitimacy to the voices in your head, as you call them, that tell you you're worthless. That she keeps you hanging on with these breadcrumbs of saying she loves you and that you can be loved, even as her primary motive is to manipulate you."

That sinks in, neatly filling the holes in my heart. I laugh without humor. "You make her sound diabolical."

"Do I?"

I sigh. "No, it's not on you. She is definitely good at fucking with my head. In fact—" I cut myself off as I think.

"Yes?"

"Just remembering something. Early on, she made an odd observation. She said I didn't want her in my head. She said it like it was a curiosity. Or a challenge."

"Now *you're* making her seem diabolical," she says, and I laugh.

"She might be. In a very ordinary way, though. And I'm no saint. I said some really ugly things to her. I hate that I did. I hate that I went to that level. It makes me think those voices in my head are right."

"Stop there. Re-state that in another way. A way that doesn't tear yourself apart."

I struggle to change my conclusion and the silence between us stretches out.

"What you're feeling is regret," she says gently. "You're feeling bad over how you behaved. The voices aren't right. You're just learning how to take responsibility for your actions. And it doesn't always feel good, Daniel. But that's okay. It's how we respond to it, how we make amends, that makes all the difference."

34

I feel a thousand times better by the time I emerge from the bar, and my spirits soar when I see the sunrise beginning to color the sky. Retaking my spot near the shoreline in front of our bungalow, I sit and watch the sun do its magic, brightening the sky in dramatic fashion.

I laugh out loud, thinking of how I had hoped being with Jules would give me some kind of stability, some kind of normalcy. That was never going to happen. For that, I need someone like Ms. Patterson. Someone who is content to sit at home and drink coffee with her cat nearby on a Sunday morning.

Fuck, there's no denying the fact that I have feelings for Ms. Patterson. Of course, I do. She knows more about me than just about anyone. Despite that, she actually seems to like me. I know it's ridiculous, but I still feel that if the circumstances were different, she and I would have a shot.

That thought is lovely but beside the point. I need to get on with things in the here and now. But first, I pull off my shirt, wrap my phone and money clip in it, and step out of my flip flops. I run into the water, diving in as soon as I'm knee-deep. The pastel colors of the sunrise reflect off the surface of the water and I simply float for a while, trying to absorb the peace and beauty of it.

Jules is sitting cross-legged on the bed when I let myself into the room. She looks up at me and a mixture of emotions travels across her face: surprise, relief, and finally anger.

Jumping up, she comes halfway to me and crosses her arms over her chest, assuming the classic defensive posture.

"Where have you been?" she asks.

"I went for a swim." I gesture to my still-wet body. I'm dripping water onto the tile floor.

"I can see that. But where were you all night? I was losing my mind waiting for you to come back."

This somehow rings false. At least the claim that she was worried all night. Because she never once called me. I have no texts from her either. More likely, she's recently woken to realize I never came back and just then started freaking out.

"I figured you were sleeping," I say. "And I needed some time away. I'm going to clean up. We've got time for breakfast before we have to get to the airport, yeah?"

"But—" She cuts herself off, unsure what she wants.

"Look," I say, moving closer to her. "I'm *really* sorry about all that last night. Truly. I should have never said what I did. Things got out of control and I regret it."

She watches me for a moment. "I thought you don't do regrets," she says with a small smile.

I laugh. "I must be changing." I said it as a reflex, but it gives me pause afterward. Because I think it might be true. I think I might be capable of change. I need her to show me she is, too, so I wait for her to say more. To apologize for the things she said and the way she behaved.

"Mind if I join you in the shower?" she asks as she unties her robe.

It's not what I was after and we both know it. "I'll be quick," I tell her. "Then it's all yours."

There are no efforts to maintain our membership in the mile-high club on our long flights back. Instead, we spend most of the time turned away from each other, sleeping. There's no hostility in how we interact, more weariness. We've done a lot to each other and we need time to recuperate.

I insist we pick up our dogs from the boarding service even though we're cutting it close to getting there on time.

My heart leaps at the sight of my boy Roscoe. His must do the same because he's all over me in an instant, jumping on me and licking me furiously. I apologize for leaving him and promise it'll never happen again, ignoring the side-eye I get from Jules over this.

I drive to Jules' house with the intention that we're just dropping her off, but she turns and looks at me when I double-park.

"I'll help with your bag," I say and jump out.

"You're not staying?"

"Not tonight, love."

She nods and hesitates before turning away.

I carry her bag to the door and wait while she unlocks it.

"I'll see you?"

It's a question I don't know how to answer, so I just give her a small nod. I'm ready to get back to the car but she pulls me into a tight hug. After a moment's hesitation, I wrap one arm around her and press a kiss to the top of her head. I reconsider leaving but only for a second. My better judgment pushes me to release her and I head home.

35

I plan to busy myself in the next week by bonding with Roscoe and taking care of little projects, including a thorough cleaning inside and out of the Porsche. I don't plan to see or speak with Jules. But I do have a makeup session with Ms. Patterson on Tuesday since I missed our regular Monday appointment.

I sense that Ms. Patterson is nervous when we meet. The long phone call we had seems to have thrown her off. It felt intimate to me, but I'm okay with that. Apparently, she isn't—at least not after the fact.

"You brought back a tan," she says with forced gaiety.

"I did. Wasn't sure it would take, actually. Last time I spent that much time in the hot sun was when I had a job in Florida and I got the worst burn."

"You worked in Florida?"

"Yeah, had a gig with a mate at this gorgeous resort right on the sand, taking care of the whims of the wealthy guests. It was a dream job, really. Lots of women on holiday looking to drink too much and slum it with the likes of me," I say with a grin. "I could have stayed there forever."

"So, what happened?"

"What do you mean?"

"Why didn't the dream job last?"

"Oh, I had to cut it short when Shay got into a mess with his girl, and I never went back to that."

She nods with a look that tells me this is about what she expected to hear, that my original description of having a job was built up to more than it actually was. It's my crutch after all—the one she identified early on, pointing out that I twist things into a version that suits me, even if that doesn't jibe with reality.

"How are things with Jules?" she asks.

"On hold, I guess you could say."

I tell her about returning to the bungalow that morning, to owning up to my bad behavior and apologizing. And that Jules did not.

"How does that make you feel?"

I roll my eyes at this sterile response. "Jesus, aren't we past that?"

"What does that mean?"

"You're being awfully careful here, Ms. Patterson. As if you want to create some kind of distance from me."

"No, I'm trying to get you to examine your feelings. That's what we do here."

"Listen, we had an especially lovely connection with that phone call, didn't we? Can't you just talk to me like we did then? With a laugh and some warmth?"

She eyes me for a moment before saying, "I don't think that's in your best interest."

"My best interest? Or yours?"

"Is there something else on your mind that we should focus on?"

Roscoe shifts and grunts, obviously picking up on my mood. I'm frustrated. Without realizing it, I came in to see Ms. Patterson with the expectation that I'd basically fall into her arms and she'd soothe me the same way she did on the phone. But now that we're back to the real world, without the distance of me being on another bloody continent, that's not going to happen.

"You know what?" I say and grab my phone from the coffee table in front of me. "I don't think I'm in the right mindset to talk. I'll see you on Thursday, yeah?" I stand, and Roscoe rouses himself as well.

Ms. Patterson puts her notepad and pen aside and stands. "You're sure that's the best decision?"

I laugh, and it comes out pathetic—sad and weary. "How the fuck would *I* know what the best decision is anyway? I'm Danny fucking Boy, amn't I? King of bad decisions."

I get as far as the door but stop when she speaks.

"That's not how I see it, Daniel. I think you're doing your best and making real strides. Don't give up on that. You've come too far."

Closing my eyes, I press my forehead against the door. I'm all twisted up with too many feelings. Feelings for Jules. Feelings for Ms. Patterson. My hand has tightened into a fist and I use it now to bang against the door because my thoughts are all about wanting the escape of heroin. I want it so bad I can taste it.

36

It's a fucking slog, but I stave off temptation over the next few weeks. Temptation for heroin, that is. I'm less successful in resisting Jules.

After four days of no contact, she texts me with a simple hello. I give it an hour and then reply asking how she is. When she suggests we meet the next day to let the dogs run at the park, I agree.

We meet at the car park and it's awkward, neither of us knowing how we should greet the other. It turns into a half-hug and her mistiming a kiss on the cheek that instead lands on my jaw.

"Shall we, then?" Jules asks, and we venture along our old route.

Walking together with careful distance between us, I wish we could erase that last night in Tulum. Turns out she feels the same because she says as much.

"I was too close to it, too injured, to acknowledge my part," she says. "But I am sorry."

The apology feels good. My steps are lighter as we go. It's hope, I realize, that we can fix this. Then she keeps talking and takes all that away.

"It was that mezcal. That stuff is deadly." She laughs softly. "It should come with a warning label: Do not drink *and* speak—only bad things will come of it."

"Ah, it was the drink, was it?" I ask.

"Maybe the spliff, too," she replies reluctantly. "A bad combination, like you've always said."

I can see there's no getting her to really take responsibility, and I don't want to go around in circles like we did before. I know by now that she won't admit to trying to take advantage of my weaknesses. She either can't or won't acknowledge how her actions prove that's exactly what she was doing. She won't change. Nor will the fact that she still has deep feelings for McManus that aren't going away anytime soon.

These things make me ready to give up on whatever it was we had. But then she turns to me and takes my hand into both of hers. In a rare show of tenderness, she brings my hand to her lips and kisses it. This is the best she can do for an apology. And so, I accept her as she is, despite all the valid reasons to end what I had already deemed a "shite relationship." Because I miss her. I miss her like I miss an addiction. Her absence is a void I don't know how to fill, so despite it being a terrible idea, I fall back in with her.

It begins again much like how it started. Her simple, sweet kiss on my hand is followed by her then grabbing me by the back of my neck to kiss me on the mouth. That chemistry we had easily reignites as I hold her in return. We stand there in the park, pressed together under the gray skies and kissing as if we're long-lost lovers finally reunited. It's that insatiable physical connection again, the one we have always relied on when substance doesn't work.

Soon, we cut short Roscoe and Molly's park run and rush back to Jules' house. Instead of going to the bedroom, we gravitate to Jules' painting room. It's the space we haven't used since that first time we were together. But it's the only place that feels right for the motives we have at the moment. After all, we are re-enacting the desperate need for each other we found when we met.

It's all about denial. Denying the truth of what we know about each other. And denying that we will ever have anything more than this sexual connection.

I've dozed off and start awake when I feel something brushing against my calf. I'm naked on the massage table, having spent myself with Jules earlier. We both got what we needed—the comfort of each other's bodies, of course, but also the pretense of closeness again.

Only, Jules isn't close now. I had wrapped her in my arms a few moments ago and now she's gone.

Then there's that tickle on my leg again.

I push up onto an elbow and see Jules. She's still nude but has a paint brush in her hand.

She's painting me.

"What's this?" I ask, amused. In all the time we've been together, the idea of her painting me has never come up.

"Just relax," she says.

After a moment, I settle back and close my eyes. The sensation of the cool brush slowly dragging across my skin is soothing. Jules had described this act with the women she works with as empowering, as showcasing their bodies as art. I wonder what she thinks this will accomplish for me. I'm not a big believer in the outside being some sort of reflection of your inner worth. But maybe she has a different plan.

"Are you painting me so I can see myself as art, or are you painting me as you see me?" I ask.

The paint brush stops, and I look at her again. She's considering the question and I can tell she hadn't thought of the difference.

"I guess we'll see," she finally says.

Once more, I relax, and she continues. But the soothing paint strokes begin to change, turning into quick slashes with multiple brushes being used for different colors. The process has turned into something other than what it started out as, and it no longer feels good.

When she announces I can sit up and look in the mirror, I do so with reluctance. I sense she has painted me as she sees me, and it's not an empowering feeling.

What I see is what I felt while she was undertaking this act: wild, unformed strokes of every color at her disposal cover my chest, torso, and legs. There is no purposeful design. It's chaos.

I think about what Ms. Patterson said when I told her Jules painted women's bodies to help them feel confident and empowered. She said Jules could be helping the women find their identities.

A scoff escapes me. Then a laugh. And another.

"What?" Jules asks, brow furrowed.

I can only hope she's better at this with the women she works with than what she did for me. Because what she did is impose her own idea of who I am onto me.

And she's wrong. This isn't the me that I now know.

This is who she thinks I am, who she wants me to be.

It's clearer than ever that we are operating with different perceptions of things. But even though that means what we're doing is going to lead to no good, I'm still not ready to put an end to it.

"It's grand," I tell her, forcing a smile. "Quite striking."

She watches me, wary for a moment before relaxing.

"Let me have a go at doing you, yeah?"

My playful tone sets her completely at ease and we entertain each other for the rest of the afternoon playing games with the paint and each other's bodies.

37

I do come clean with Ms. Patterson about all this, though, and she doesn't try to hide her disappointment.

"You're saying you'll keep on with her even though you know it's not a healthy relationship?" she asks.

"Yes, that's what I'm saying. Gotta have some vices, don't I?"

I'm in a combative mood. I knew Ms. Patterson would lay bare all the reasons why this is a bad idea, but I just don't want to hear it from her. I suppose I could have lied to her, or omitted the truth of being back with Jules, but I have motives in telling her the truth that will come out soon enough.

"Smoking is a vice. Drinking is a vice," she says. "Being with a woman who has abused your trust and disregarded your sobriety is more than a vice. It is self-destructive."

I roll my eyes. "Honey, you have no idea the ways I can self-destruct. This ain't it."

"Ms. Patterson."

"What?"

"You are to call me Ms. Patterson. You know that."

"Yeah yeah."

Silence overtakes us for several long minutes.

"You don't seem terribly happy in being with her again," she finally says. "Or is there something else you'd like to talk about."

"Maybe *you're* the one who's not terribly happy that I'm with her?" I suggest and she stares at me blankly. "Go on, you can admit to being just a wee bit jealous, can't you? It may not be the 'professional' thing to do, but it's okay. I won't tell anyone." I give her a wink.

"Daniel—"

"Danny Boy."

"What?"

"I've been trying to get you to understand for months that I am Danny Boy. That's who I am. That's what *you* should call *me*."

This flusters her. I'm regressing before her eyes and she's put off.

"Come on, *Ms.* Patterson," I say. "I expect more from you! You should know how to handle me by now. Go on, put me in my place. Reveal me to myself like you've done before. Tell me something like when you said I lost my identity. That was a real winner, wasn't it?"

She looks down at her notepad and taps the end of her pen against the spiral binding.

I wait.

Finally, she meets my eyes, her gaze steady. "I won't be giving you permission to make bad decisions, Daniel."

"Ah, is that the diagnosis? Seems pretty shallow, really."

"You have come too far to play this game now."

"Game?"

"I know what you're doing. Do not play me for a fool."

As usual, she sees right through me. I've been pushing her, trying to convince her I'm allowed to do the wrong thing because I'm *Danny Boy*—as if that is some kind of excuse. I want to apologize. I want to throw myself at her mercy and beg for her to help me because I know I'm going backwards by being with Jules again. But I can't. The best I can do is try to deflect.

"You are not the fool in this scenario," I say. "You are my queen and I bow to you." I get up and literally bow in front of her, complete with arm sweeping out before resting my hand on my heart.

"That's enough," she says.

"My dear Ms. Patterson, if you can't give me permission for my bad decision to be with Jules, then what advice would you give me to try to make it something worthwhile?

I can see the relief in her face with my change in attitude, and she sets about methodically detailing how I should manage my relationship going forward. She insists that I establish some boundaries with Jules this time around. She says I should eliminate or limit drinking alcohol when we're together, that I should go back to attempting to have real dates, rather than staying in so much, and that I should try to focus on communicating with words rather than resorting to sex.

It's all reasonable and I agree to it in theory. Making it happen is another matter.

38

J ust like before, Jules proves to be a distraction for me. I had
   stopped going to NA meetings when I first got in deep with
   Jules and never returned. The only thing I kept up with then
and continue now are my sessions with Ms. Patterson. Time slips by
before I realize I've ignored the one thing my brother asked of me—
checking up on Martin. When Shay reminds me of that task, I apologize profusely and promise to get right on it.

Martin has three boys, each wilder than the next. They've always
seemed to be these tornado-like forces, so full of energy and motion.
So, it doesn't surprise me when all three rush to beat each other in
answering my knock on the front door of their house.

"Danny Boy!" Sean—the littlest one—shouts.

"Hello, lads," I say. "And what are you lot up to?"

"Ma is making us do laundry and other cleanup," Donal—the
oldest one—says with a sour look on his mug.

"Ah, mind your Ma," I say. "I'm sure she appreciates your help.
Now, where's your Da?"

"At his other house. Where do you think?" Colm—the middle one—says.

"Other house?"

Celia comes to the door then, rag and dust spray in hand. "Go on, boys, back to your chores," she tells them.

"But—" Sean starts in a whine.

"Listen to your Ma," I say. "One day you'll realize how lucky you are to have a mother who works alongside you to make a nice home."

"Eh, yeah, right," Donal says reluctantly, and the boys head off with lackluster waves goodbye to me.

"How are you, Celia?" I ask.

"Been better. You're looking for Marty, then? Don't you know he's done this temporary moving out thing? Has a rented house just a few blocks from here."

She says it matter of fact, like she has no patience for an explanation, but that doesn't stop my surprise. I knew the guy had committed some major fuck-ups, as detailed in the tabloids, but it's still hard to conceive of the idea that these two would have separated. They have been married longer than any couple I know.

"I'm sorry to hear—" I start but she cuts me off. She doesn't want to hear my thoughts on the matter or give me any more details other than Marty's new address.

———

Martin's rental is nice enough on the outside, but it has a distinctly "divorced dad" feel on the inside. It's sparsely furnished, with nothing on the walls, and no real character. Seems he's spent all his time in the gym rather than making this a real home. He's transformed himself over the last six months or so into a different person. Gone is the baby fat, replaced by a Chris Evans-like physique. He was the last holdout of the band, the last one to seem like a regular guy. What with Conor being Mr. Perfect, Gavin having adopted an athletic build, and my brother being in fighting shape so he can conquer the drums,

Martin was always the one to feel like he could be your mate down at the pub. Now he's turned into bloody Captain America.

"Your temporary digs?" I ask him once we're seated on the sofa.

"Long-term temporary, I guess," he says. "Until I find something I want to buy."

"Ah. Well, your ex there seems to think this isn't going to last. Said it was a temporary move out."

Martin sighs and shakes his head. "She'd be happy for me to come right back, but it's not happening."

"You on to one of those lovelies from the tabloid stories I saw?"

He goes stiff with the directness of my question. I'm not one to beat around the bush, so he shouldn't have expected anything less.

"What do you want, Danny Boy?"

"I, em, I dunno," I say with a laugh. I hadn't given much thought to concocting a story about why I was visiting him. "Guess I'm just restless. You know, being off tour."

His defensive posture loosens as he sits back. "What are you doing with your time, then?"

"Ah, little bit of this and that," I reply evasively.

"Well, I'm sure you'll be glad to have Shay back for a spell?"

"Back? What do you mean?"

"Gavin and Conor want to go to studio. Did Shay not tell you he'll be back in a week or so?"

Shay hadn't mentioned that. I wonder if he was hoping to surprise me by showing up unannounced just to see if I was getting myself into any kind of trouble. And, of course, I am doing just that by still seeing Jules. But he has no idea about her as far as I can tell. For reasons I can't quite figure, neither Gavin nor Conor has told my brother about Jules.

"That's good news," I say. "I'm eager for you all to get on with it and back on tour."

"Keep your patience on that. Still a ways to go."

"Maybe I'll sit in on the studio stuff with you guys."

"It'll bore you to tears. Why don't you take the time to get out and travel or something? I was just in London. It's a quick trip but it still feels like getting away."

My Tulum tan has long since faded, and no one knows I was even there, so I won't be mentioning it now.

"What was in London?"

Martin straightens up and looks conflicted before admitting, "A girl."

"You stud, you," I tease, and he laughs.

"Well, it was a one-off. I don't expect to see her again."

There's disappointment in his voice and the distant look in his eyes reveals a distinct longing. My relationship situation doesn't provoke the same kind of feelings. That moment of connection—of *love*—I felt for Jules on our last full day in Tulum has morphed into the same elusive feeling you get from a good dream you wake from and can never recapture. Jules and I are in an odd state now. I know I'm hanging onto something with her that I shouldn't. I just can't seem to break away.

"How did you know it was over with Celia," I blurt out.

Martin laughs, surprised. "You come right out with it, don't you?"

"Why not?"

"Why the fuck not, indeed." He pauses and looks toward the kitchen for a long moment.

There isn't much there to keep his interest. Not so much as a fruit bowl adorns the countertop.

"I suppose I knew without really knowing for a long while," he says. "It just came to a point where I realized that I couldn't be myself with her. You know, she was stuck on an old version of me she didn't want to let go, no matter how much I had changed. So, really, it was something sort of bubbling under the surface. It just needed to come to a boil with time, so to speak."

"Ashley *is* hot," I say with a laugh, breezing by the point he's made about how he changed. That will only resonate with me later. For now, it's tucked away in my subconscious.

Martin looks at me mournfully. "I fucked around with her, but she wasn't the reason for all this." He gestures to his spare living space.

"Didn't hurt, though, yeah?"

I laugh again, and he stares at me, exasperated. It's a look I've elicited more than any other in my life. But then he throws up his hands and lets loose a laugh at his own expense. Marty's always been quick to roll with a joke, even if he's the punchline. Only, something feels different now. It feels like he's in on the joke in a way he hasn't been before. He may be sitting his arse in a sad-sack house, separated from his wife, but he seems . . . happy. Seeing he can be happy when he's left his relationship behind makes me wonder once more what the fuck I'm doing with Jules.

39

We're out to dinner when I tell Jules that Shay is coming into town. I've forced this date as a way to keep from slipping back into our old routine of either drinking at home or going out to places like Jacob's club where there will surely be too much temptation.

I might have overcorrected, however, because when I came up short for what to do, I ended up recreating what Ms. Patterson did when I stalked her that time. So, here we are, sitting awkwardly in The Marker Hotel's Brassiere restaurant, with tickets to see bloody *Spamalot* afterward. Jules was gamely going along with this, even though it's not her scene. That changes when I mention my brother's name.

"And is he coming just to visit you?" she asks carefully.

"Nah. He and the guys are going into studio."

"So soon? They just finished—" she cuts herself off.

I sigh. "Yes, they just barely finished the tour, I know." It's that over-familiarity slipping through again. She knows exactly when the band ended their tour because she's been keeping tabs, despite how she tries to act beyond it all.

"Well, I'm sure you'll be glad to see Shay."

"Yes, of course." I hesitate. This is the part I haven't been eager to get to. "Thing is, when he's here, I'll be . . . occupied."

She eyes me. "Occupied?"

"Well, you know. With helping the band. I have a mind to be in the studio with them, to see what I might be able to learn from those goings on."

"Those sessions can be very time consuming," she allows, and I relax a degree. But that reprieve disappears when she continues. "I spent plenty of my life there—both for my own recordings and with Gavin when they were recording."

With Gavin.

Since our blowout fight, she's dropped any effort of not mentioning her past relationship with Gavin and Rogue. It hasn't been constant, mind, but it's *very* noticeable.

"Well, I'll get to see for myself. This will be the first time I've been around when they recorded, so it'll be interesting to see the process. Though Marty tells me I'll be bored to tears," I say with a laugh.

That reference stops her mid-bite and she lowers her forkful of salmon. "Do you . . . hang out with the guys?"

"Outside of the tour? No, not really. They've always been Shay's mates."

"But, wait. You said you saw Gavin—to talk about *me*." She lets that hang in the air for a moment, but I don't take the bait. There's no way I'm going to feel guilty about that, especially given that he was absolutely right about his warning to me. She continues, "And didn't you say something about Conor and motorbike lessons?"

"Yeah. Reminds me, I really need to get a bike."

Ignoring that, she says, "And now you just saw Martin?"

"Shay asked me to check up on him. But, yeah, we ended up having a laugh together."

"That sounds like mates to me."

I shrug dismissively. None of this seems relevant to what I need to tell her. "Anyway," I say, "I just mean to tell you that I think I mightn't be in touch very much while Shay's here."

"I could always visit you there at the studio."

The idea of her dropping in to see what kind of trouble she can stir up with Gavin has me scrambling to put her off. But she keeps at it before I can think of something to say.

"Seeing how you were going to talk to Shay on my behalf about getting back into the industry."

Me and my stupid gob. What was I thinking ever suggesting that? I was in some sort of love-sick haze, is what. I thought I'd found what I needed with Jules. All because of a spell cast while swimming in the Mexican ocean in the rain. I hadn't thought twice about it after our epic fight, just sort of assumed we both knew it was an offer no longer on the table. Not so for Jules, it seems.

"About that," I say, "I don't think now is the time to approach it."

She raises an eyebrow. "No? Seems terribly convenient with him being back here and in studio."

I have no doubt she reads this for what it is. She knows I don't want her there, but she's enjoying making me squirm in response. Best to just get to the heart of the matter, even if I know it will sting a bit.

"Well, he doesn't even know I'm seeing you, so it'd be a pretty big fucking leap to make at this point."

It takes her a second to digest this news. And when she does, I can see my blow has landed exactly as I thought it would.

"But, I'm the one you love," she says with phony sweetness. "How can you not have told your brother about your *love?*"

It's a jab that pisses me off. Again, I'm learning how to truly regret my actions. It's a new and unwelcome feeling. I wish I had never told her I loved her. I wish I had never told her I'd talk to Shay on her behalf. But I have and now she's only too happy to use my words against me. Jesus, it feels like all connecting with someone gets you is manipulation in return.

"Just don't, Jules," I say wearily.

"Don't worry. I'm only too happy to leave you on your own. In fact, let's start with that right away, shall we?"

Dropping her napkin over her half-eaten entree, she stands and gathers her purse.

"Really? *This* is where you're drawing the line? Over me not having told Shay? Or is it over me not wanting to ask him to help you?"

"I should have never taken up with you to begin with. We both know that."

I can feel the eyes all around us, watching this end to us play out.

"What about the show?" I ask lamely. It feels like I should make some sort of effort to keep her, even if a part of me is relieved for her to be breaking things off.

"Fuck your stupid show *and* your weak attempts to live a boring existence. You will never be happy living the straight life. You know that, right?"

She may be right, but I have no desire for her, of all people, to make this assertion. Still, I remain calm and I'm pleased that I'm not tempted to flip the table or send a wine glass flying. That version of me existed not too long ago. The one that would do things without real thought, just to get a reaction. That might have generated fleeting excitement, but this "boring existence" has offered me something more rewarding: a sense of peace. It's peace because I realize the negativity in my head hasn't found its foothold the way it so easily used to. Nor have I succumbed to using the low expectations others had of me as a way to justify turning to heroin like I've done in the past. What's made the difference? Maybe it's because now I have Ms. Patterson's support.

The bottom line is that Jules hasn't helped with either of these things. She has only ever stirred up the darkness in my head and she's only ever played to my worst instincts—desperate to resurrect and manipulate the remnants of my old self. This is made abundantly clear by her declaring I'll be miserable with a normal life.

"My dear therapist would call that projection, you know?" I ask with a laugh and sit back in my leather club chair.

"You know what I *still* think about that situation," she says pointedly.

"Yeah, well, you were right with your first guess." I shouldn't let her goad me, especially knowing that's what she's after. But nobody's perfect, least of all me. "I *do* want to fuck her."

I hear some gasps. The restaurant's tables are too damn close together, so we have been giving the crowd a show in addition to their pre-theater meal.

"Just try not to call her *Mammy* when you do, yeah?"

I laugh. It was a good comeback, I have to admit. My genuine smile makes her hesitate. She's been on the verge of turning on heel and stalking out and now she relaxes a degree. The corner of her mouth turns up. That's the thing, we've always, on some base level, understood each other. That's why it was so easy to go back with her —because her first argument for why we should be together to begin with, that we were the kind of fucked-up that only we could under-stand, still holds true.

Still, I'm ready to let this twisted connection go.

"Take care of yourself, okay Jules?" I tell her softly.

She takes a deep breath and I catch her blinking back tears. "You, too."

Once she's gone, I relax. I'm ready to dig back into my steak dinner but realize I'm still being watched.

"Oy," I call out. "I have an extra ticket to the show. Any takers?"

Shaking my head, I laugh again. It feels good to have resisted falling right back into it with Jules. I feel a sort of calm descend over me, which is a foreign fucking sensation. But also, one I think I've earned.

40

"My dear Ms. Patterson, you will be so proud of me," I say as soon as she's closed her office door behind me and Roscoe. "And why is that?"

I sink into my chair and Roscoe does his usual thing of turning around in a circle a couple times before leaning up against my leg.

"I made a bona fide *good* decision."

My enthusiasm and good humor is hard to mistake. It seems to rub off on her, too, because she's gifting me with a warm smile.

"It's lovely to see you so proud of *yourself*," she says.

"I am that, indeed. In fact, I may not even need to continue these sessions since I've got things so well sorted."

That earns me a dubious stare and I laugh.

"Really, though. Shame it will cost you my business. Oh, and that idea I had of getting you a new client in the form of Martin Whelan isn't going to work out either, sorry to say."

"No?" Her smile has returned, and it's bemused.

"Nah, turns out that guy has his head on straight. Wouldn't think so what with all the tabloid drama, but I saw him the other day and he's doing just fine. It surprised me, actually. Here I was, thinking he'd be devastated. I mean, all I've ever known him as is this married guy with kids. Turns out there was more depth going on there. He said he needed to sort of break away from his wife in order to just be himself. And it must have been the right thing because he looked happy, I have to say."

After a moment of absorbing this, she says, "Well, go on, tell me about this good decision of yours."

I tell her everything about my date with Jules last evening, including how I stole the restaurant and theater idea. She finds that last bit mildly amusing but isn't sold on my claim that Jules and I are officially and totally over.

"Your whole time with Jules has seen you conflicted—about her motives and your motives. You got back together after what anyone else would have found to have been irreparable harm done with that fight in Tulum. What makes you say this is different?"

"It *feels* different. I dunno why."

She watches me, letting the silence stretch out to encourage me to produce an answer rather than just brush it off. That's the point, after all, of being here in this room together—to examine things.

"I guess," I say after a spell, "that warning Gavin gave me finally clicked."

"Remind me what he said?"

"It was that Jules was only interested in what was good for her. That she was an opportunist. I didn't really take it to heart, honestly, because it sort of felt like he was talking about me. I mean, for fuck's sake, hasn't that been my whole life? Only doing what would serve me?"

"It *was*."

She emphasizes the past tense and I nod slowly. It's hard to believe I'm not that guy anymore.

"Okay," she continues, "so you recognized yourself in Jules from the start and didn't want to reject her out of hand because doing so would have meant what?"

"I dunno." My good mood is slipping away with this discussion. Wasn't it enough to have done the right thing by ending it with Jules? Why do we have to rehash everything else? It's times like these where

Ms. Patterson pushes me beyond my comfort zone that I wish I'd never started with her.

"Could it have been what we talked about before? That if you rejected her, you'd be rejecting that version of yourself and then be left with not knowing what your identity was?"

"This again?"

"Well, why not?"

"Because I'm fucking sick of it," I snap.

She takes a deep breath and presses her hands against her notepad. "Let me ask you something," she says. "How would your friends describe you?"

"Friends?" I scoff.

"Yes. Your friends: Gavin, Martin, and Conor."

"They're Shay's friends."

"I think you should re-exam that. I mean, just think about what you've told me. Gavin gave you his honest advice about Jules. He told you those personal things about himself to get across a warning in order to protect *you*. And Martin opened up to you about what ended his marriage. That was also incredibly personal. It shows a degree of trust in you."

I shake my head, not ready to accept her generous reading of what those lads are about when it comes to me. "And what has Conor supposedly done to show his friendship?"

"Well, he gave you his time with the motorbike lesson, didn't he? Even though you admit to having betrayed his trust before. He didn't give up on you."

"I wouldn't go that far. They're all Shay's mates. They've come to tolerate me for his sake."

Despite my denial, her depiction of the friendship these guys have shown stays with me. I've never considered that I would have a connection with those guys on my own, without Shay factoring in. But they have all been amazingly welcome of me, even Mr. Perfect who has every reason to keep me at arm's length.

Ms. Patterson laughs softly and shakes her head.

"What?"

"It's just, you've made such great strides in our sessions. You are really adept at analyzing your feelings and have come to understand how your decisions have consequences. But the one thing that hasn't changed is your absolute disbelief that you could really matter to someone else."

"Can't expect miracles, here, can we?" I ask with a wink.

"I'm going to ignore you *again* trying to deflect with a joke, Daniel," she says with strained patience. "The reason Gavin and Conor, and Martin gave you those things is because that's what friends do. It's really *not* what anyone does out of obligation."

Though it's a lovely thought, her insistence on this issue baffles me. "What was your point with all this, anyway?" I ask.

"I suppose it's to prove to you that another element of progress you've made is in connecting with others. You have people you can call your friends. I imagine they would describe you as a friend, as well."

I laugh at the new and improved diagnosis. It's a far cry from where I once was. "I'm cured, then, am I?"

"Let's not get ahead of ourselves," she replies with a smile. "There's always more work to be done."

"Over a pint, though, maybe?" I figure it can't hurt to try.

"Oh, look," she says, "our time is up for today. Until next time."

I stand and stretch. Roscoe does the same. I feel drained from this session. But also, lighter. It's a good feeling.

"One of these days, Ms. Patterson, I'm going to take you for a drink. And it will be a grand thing, indeed."

She smiles, but pivots, saying, "You came in here proud of yourself, saying I'd be proud of you, too. I am proud of you. Good work, Daniel."

I can't help a huge smile from taking over my face. And for the first time in a very long time, I feel like Daniel, not Danny Boy.

41

I pick up Shay from the airport even though he didn't ask for the favor. I figure it's the least I can do, what with all he's done for me. I know exactly what he's doing when he eyes me. He's trying to gauge whether I'm clean or not. That suspicion isn't something I'll likely ever escape, not even if I'm sober for the rest of my life.

During the drive, he confirms what I assumed about his living situation—his move to San Francisco is permanent. He is committed to making a life with Jessica and that means being there. It's made him a happy man, so I can't deny him that. Still, the timing is a bitch. I've only just recently reestablished a relationship with the kid, and then he goes and moves halfway around the world. He suggests Roscoe and I visit him over there, but I get the feeling that offer hasn't been pre-approved by his better half. I've come between the two of them before, so I'm wary of becoming a problem again. I have to give myself credit for such forethought. Or maybe, I should give Ms. Patterson credit for that. Hooking up with her was the best thing I've done in my life. I can't imagine having the same kind of connection with any other therapist.

I want to tell Shay all about her. I want to tell him what a godsend she's been, how much she's helped me, and that I adore her beyond our client-therapist relationship. I want to tell him about the nearly five-hour phone call she and I shared when I was in Tulum and needed a voice of reason and comfort. But I can't admit to any of that.

Instead, once home, Shay inspects his house as if expecting to find I've trashed it. When he realizes I haven't turned the place into a drug den and that it's actually in tip-top form, he relaxes and we settle into the Man Cave with some beers.

"So, what do you think of me joining you lads in studio?" I ask. "I've never seen the process. It could be a real kick."

"Yeah, sure. Just stay out of the way," Shay tells me.

"What? No guest starring on the album for me?" I tease as I straddle the stool at Shay's drum kit. I take the sticks and hold one each in my fists.

Shay rolls his eyes. "Fuck's sake, don't hold them like that."

"This isn't right?" I tap on the skins awkwardly.

"If your aim is to have a wank, then that'll do."

I laugh. "What if my aim is to actually do it proper like?"

I'm pleased when Shay responds by helping me with the correct way to handle the drumsticks. He's always been hyper-cautious when it comes to the instrument that has been both his passion and his livelihood. But for some reason I can't pinpoint, tonight is different. Tonight, we stay up until four in the morning as he patiently teaches me some basics while we talk and drink. It isn't until we're headed to our separate rooms to go to sleep that I realize how much I missed the kid. He has always brought out the best in me.

———

We get to the studio at eleven, after too little sleep and only a cup of coffee to get us going. This doesn't seem to matter to Shay. He's pumped, and his energy is contagious.

Rogue has recorded in this same studio since they started. It looks to have been recently renovated, though, as the enormous angled soundboard filling the front room, along with the computer and monitor at its center, is new technology. The walls have a fresh coat of white paint and the place smells conspicuously clean, as if someone made special preparations for the band's arrival. They are practically royalty in the music business, so I guess that treatment makes sense.

Shay introduces me to the yokes at the soundboard, two engineers they've worked with for many years. There's no need for their long-time producer Roger Ahern to be here for these early sessions. Large speakers are amplifying the guitar Conor is playing in the hardwood floor sound booth we can see to the left.

Of course, Mr. Perfect would already be here. He's got headphones on but is his normal well-styled self in a white tee shirt that clings to his chest under a red and white plaid flannel and black jeans.

"Better late than never, Seamus!"

We turn to see Gavin arriving, his eyes bright and a playful grin on his face. This isn't their first day in the studio. Apparently, Gavin was too eager to start and couldn't wait for Shay to come in, so they had him on video chat from San Francisco yesterday while they tinkered with new ideas.

"Fuck off," Shay tells him without malice, and the two hug.

It never ceases to amaze me that these guys embrace each other so often. They've known each other since they were only little, spend more time together than is healthy, and still like each other.

"DB, good to see you," Gavin says. He surprises me by giving me a quick hug. As he pulls away he meets my eyes. "Everything good with you?"

It's clear as day to me what he means. He's asking about Jules. I just hope Shay doesn't read anything more into the inquiry because I don't want him to know about all that.

"Yeah, good," I say. "Just here to see how it all works."

"Cool. Glad to have you."

He claps me on the back as he starts to move past me. Then he stops abruptly and turns back. "Oh, fair warning, mates—I have to cut out at about four o'clock."

"You wanker," Shay says. "After giving me such a hard time about not being here yesterday?"

Gavin laughs. "Yeah, well. I'm taking Sophie for a night out. She's finally past that morning sickness thing, so I want to treat her to something special."

"If it's for Sophie, then okay," Shay says.

My brother has some sort of connection with Sophie, which is evident in how easily he's changed his attitude now.

"Where will you take her?" I ask, and all eyes turn to me.

I suppose it's an odd question coming from me. But my recent dating fails have left me curious at what other people do.

"Eh, well, I'll tell you, it's dead romantic like. I've got a plane chartered to take us to Venice. Got a nice dinner and hotel set up there. We'll be back after lunch tomorrow."

I should have known Gavin wouldn't be doing something normal. He and Sophie are not your average couple.

"Sounds lovely," Martin says, joining us. "Daisy going with you?"

"No, she'll stay with the nanny. Just a quick trip," Gavin says. "Anyway, let's get to it."

As is their habit, the guys all fall in line when Gavin makes his requests of them. He's the lead singer for a reason.

———

I spend the rest of the day in the studio, leaning over the shoulders of the sound engineers, picking their brains for how the dozens of sliders on the board affect things. It fascinates me, and I soak it all up, sensing a new addiction could be upon me. Maybe it makes more sense to try to learn this side of things. I might be getting too old to climb those lighting rigs, anyway.

Though the guys are deep into piecing together a new song based around the guitar line Conor had been playing when we got there, Gavin is good on his word and leaves at four. The rest of us take the opportunity to order in food. As I join in on the fish and chips, I realize that they're all treating me like it's a given that I should be there. I feel like one of them, part of something bigger than myself. And fuck that feels good—to *not* be concerned with only myself. Thinking back, I realize this was the attitude when we were all on tour, but I had always assumed that vibe had an expiration date on it. I figured once the tour was over, so too would be the inclusion they offered. I'm only now realizing that once these guys have given their friendship, it's not easily lost. Even for me.

We're all gathered around the sofas and chairs that sit in front of the soundboard, using the scarred wood coffee table to eat off. I look around at Conor, Martin, and Shay. They're engaged in an easy banter, never at a loss for conversation, whether it's about their recent travels, sports, new music they've discovered, or anything in between. Shay was right about them being his brothers. What luck to have found them.

"And what have you been doing with yourself, Danny Boy?" Shay asks me. "I haven't been very good at keeping in touch."

"Hmm?" The question catches me off guard. My head had been elsewhere, but I also don't know what to say. I glance at Conor and he's watching me with interest. Martin is occupied with opening another bottle of Smithwick's Ale.

"Can't say I've done a whole lot," I hedge.

And then, as if she'd orchestrated the timing of this herself, Jules lets herself into the studio.

42

"Hello, fellas," she says with a nod.

The guys all stand to greet her. I do not. I stay where I am and scramble to think what the fuck I'm going to say. And how I'm going to get her out of here before she embarrasses me in front of my brother.

"Haven't seen you in forever, Julia," Martin says.

"Julia," Conor says.

Shay gives her a smile.

Then everyone waits. Waits for her to say something. Waits for me to stand and join them. I still don't make a move.

"Looks like I caught you at a good time. Dinner break?" she says. But her eyes travel beyond the group, searching. She's not here to fuck with me. She's not here to try to force a way back into the music industry. She's here to see Gavin.

I finally stand and shuffle closer. I feel Conor watching me before turning his gaze to Shay, then back to me.

"Yeah, we're just grabbing a quick bite before starting back up," Conor says.

"Gavin's not here," I say.

Shay looks at me curiously for volunteering this information but doesn't say anything.

"No?" she asks.

"He left early. Won't be back tonight."

Jules takes a moment before responding. I can see she's conflicted. She had probably come here hoping to stir things up and Gavin's absence has thwarted that plan. Would it be worth her while to out me instead? My confession that I hadn't told Shay about her is something she could use against me and we both know it. She could easily air all our dirty laundry at this very moment and in doing so drive a wedge between me and my brother. And she'd do it for the same reason she did all the other destructive acts where I was concerned—to exploit my weaknesses and make herself feel empowered.

"Well, he's not who I came to see—" she starts but Conor interrupts her.

"You still singing, Julia?" he asks.

"Eh, no. I stepped away from all that some years ago."

"That's a shame. You ever want to try your hand at it again, you can call on us."

I'm confused by Conor's generous offer. But when I see the way it makes Jules smile, how she's beaming at the idea, I realize Conor was deliberately dangling a shiny object in front of her to distract her from what she was obviously about to do. Instead of allowing her to reveal our history, he's preying upon her ambitions to make it clear that she has a choice in how she proceeds. If she chooses to try to lash out at me, she would lose any offer from Conor to help her later.

"That's so sweet. Really appreciate that," she says, and I breathe a sigh of relief.

"Well, we should get back to it," Conor says.

"Oh, right, sure," she says. She smiles and nods, and then she locks eyes with me. "Maybe you can let Gav know I came by? I still think about him, you know?"

God, she's cruel. So much so that I can't help but smile. "He's taken his wife on this lovely romantic getaway for the night. But we can mention it when he's back," I say.

She holds back a laugh. There's no misunderstanding what we've done—it's one final jab at each other. A confirmation that though we weren't good together, we did understand each other.

"Take care, lads," she says and shows herself out.

———

When Shay and Martin go back to their instruments, Conor stays behind.

"You all right, then?" he asks.

I nod. "Thanks for that, man. That whole thing is done and over. I . . . I guess you know I never told Shay?"

"Appeared that way."

"Why didn't you or Gav ever say anything?"

"Not our business. And I think you asked us both to keep it quiet, right?"

"Yeah, but—"

"When a friend needs your confidence, that's what you give him," Conor says and nods to put the matter to rest.

"I just . . . I don't understand."

"What?"

"I've fucked you over, Conor. Why would you go out of your way for me?"

Conor watches me for a moment. "Don't you know?"

"Know what?"

"Whether I like it or not, you're one of us, Danny Boy."

"I know I'm a pain—"

"You're one of us," he repeats. "It's as simple as that. It means that whatever fuck ups you commit, that's not something that's going to get you cut lose. We'd all of us be on the outs if we allowed that sort of thing to ruin us."

Like Gavin earlier, Conor claps me on the back. There's an incredible sense of reassurance in it.

43

It's just past nine o'clock when Shay takes a call on his cell. We're all still in the studio but had been winding down. I can see my brother through the glass, but I can't hear his side of the conversation through the speakers, since the engineers muted the sound to give him privacy. It's clear enough Shay is reluctantly agreeing to something and I wonder if Jessica is on the line, talking about hopping on a plane to join him here. That would disappoint me, I have to admit. I'm quite enjoying this time with Shay.

But when he comes out to the front room, he announces that Gavin has asked him to go to his house to relieve the nanny who has fallen ill with food poisoning.

"He says Daisy is down for the night, that he just needs someone to be there when she wakes in the morning," Shay explains to me, Conor and Martin. "Says they'll come back earlier than planned tomorrow."

Martin laughs. "Why'd he call you, do you suppose?"

"He's Daisy's godfather," Conor says. There's a trace of bitterness in his voice that he can't hide and I suspect it has something to do with the still not-quite-healed rift in his and Gavin's friendship. Sleeping with your best friend's wife will do that.

"That, and I suspect Sophie's trying to be clever," Shay says. "She's dying for me and Jessica to join the baby club."

"Well, you enjoy the gig, yeah?" I tell my brother.

"Fuck that. You're coming with me, Danny Boy."

———

The nanny looks positively green with nausea and is gone in a flash once we arrive.

"So," Shay says, "I guess we should look in on Daisy?"

"Why are you asking me? I know exactly nothing about kids," I tell him.

"Let's go."

He leads me down the hall and finds the right door. Daisy's room is decorated in soothing shades of cream with pink accents. There are photos of Gavin on the wall at her eye-level so she can gaze upon him while in her crib. That must have been something Sophie did while he was away on tour so that the kid could feel like her Dad was around. She's sleeping peacefully now, on her back, in the crib she's on her way to outgrowing.

"Should I take a picture of her," Shay whispers, "to send to Gav? Let him know all is well?"

"I dunno. Is that creepy?"

"How about if I stick my head in the shot? So, it's like 'I'm here' and she's okay?"

I laugh, and he shushes me. "That sounds even creepier. Fuck's sake, just text him that we're here."

Nodding, he turns and starts typing on his phone as he leaves the room.

We make ourselves comfortable in the living room, finding that there is a video baby monitor on the coffee table between us. We can see and hear Daisy via an ingenious night vision camera stationed somewhere in her room. I've got the better seat on the sofa, facing the wall of windows looking out to the sea. The lights of the Dalkey coastline are lighting up the night and it's a spectacular view.

Once Shay's had his say with some back and forth texts, he puts down his phone and looks at me.

"So," he says, "you've been fucking Julia O'Flaherty, have you?"

"What? No," I lie, and he just stares at me. "I mean—fucking Quinn. He *did* tell you."

I should have known he was bullshitting me with all that hearts and flowers friendship nonsense.

"No, Conor didn't tell me about her, and now I have to wonder about that, too."

"Well, then," I stammer, "how did you know?"

"Because I've got two fucking eyes, haven't I? It couldn't have been clearer, just being in the same room as you two."

"Oh." I relax and reconsider my condemnation of Quinn. I guess he was telling the truth. And now I have to really accept what he said about me being one of them. That is, unless my brother is angry enough to want me to steer clear of his group of friends after this.

"But I take it whatever you had is over now? That much was obvious, as well."

"Completely over and done," I agree enthusiastically.

Shay is quiet as he watches me. "What all went on with that?" he finally asks.

I give him the abbreviated version, focusing mostly on the fact that we both knew, in the end, that we weren't compatible. That's a whitewashing of the truth, I know, but I never did want to admit to Shay all the ways I was looking for trouble with Jules. He would see it as proof for his need to worry about me and feel the need to return home, jeopardizing his relationship with Jessica once again.

"Was she after you to get to Gavin?" he asks when I've concluded.

Though it's the exact same question I had at the beginning of my time with Jules, and many times after that, I'm offended that Shay has the same thought.

"What, am I not attractive? I thought I was pulling off a better look these days."

"Don't try to be cute about this, Danny Boy. I'm asking because I need to know if she's a threat to my band."

Of course, that would be his priority. Shay has always made it clear his band is the most important thing to him, giving me short shrift in the process.

"How's about caring about your dear brother first off?" I ask, unable to resist falling back on my tried and true method of guilt-tripping my baby brother. It's a tactic I used often over the years, mostly when I needed money or his time to help me when I bottomed out. I haven't felt the need to do this in a long time, however, and it leaves a bad taste in my mouth. It feels cheap, like it's . . . beneath me.

"You should be thinking in the same terms," Shay continues, ignoring my attempt at manipulating him, "now that you have a real interest in Rogue."

"What's that mean?"

"It means, you're part of the crew, aren't you? We rely on you. I should think you'd want to be sure we're solid—if only for your own sake."

"Well, yeah, I do want that. I'd never do anything to threaten the band, Shay. Don't you know that?"

He gives me a look of disbelief that I don't quite track.

"You think I would?" I ask.

"I think you *have*, that's the thing. Like when you stole Conor's guitar?"

Thinking back on that escapade makes me laugh. It was one of those things I did on impulse. I just grabbed the guitar right out of the storage unit that was being packed up at the end of the tour. At first, I just wanted to have a closer look at it. Then, I realized no one was around, so I walked it right out of the Dublin 3Arena. Once I had it in hand, I knew I couldn't really keep it. But giving it back seemed more dangerous than what I ended up doing, which was trying to sell it. That turned into quite the cockup. Mr. Perfect nearly lost his legendary cool, he was so angry with me.

"That's ancient history," I say. It does feel like forever ago. I recognize that behavior, but I don't identify with it anymore, if that makes any sense.

"Then there's the time when you came crashing into me and broke my fucking wrist."

The vision of slipping off the ladder and swinging wildly down onto Shay at his kit flashes in my mind. Again, I can't help but laugh. I did know how to make things interesting.

"Always a laugh, yeah?" Shay asks wearily. He's tired. Exhausted, actually. He came in from the States and never properly rested to rid himself of jet lag. Now this to further burden him.

"Listen, you have nothing to worry about. I know you can't help yourself, but I'm not after hurting the band. I *won't* hurt the band."

Shay watches me silently, dubiously.

"Honestly. For the first time in I don't know how long, I feel invested in something. That's you lot. And I will do everything I can not to fuck it up."

It takes a moment, but finally the expression on his face morphs into relief. I'm sure mine does, too.

44

A sharp rapping noise startles me awake. I'm completely disoriented as I wipe drool from my mouth. I see Shay asleep in the chair across from me. Dead to the world, he sits with head lolled to the side, arms slack on the armrests and legs spread wide. I slowly realize that we're at Gavin's. The full reason for this escapes me, however, as I stretch out on the sofa, closing my eyes to return to sleep.

The noise starts up again, though, and my eyes fly open, landing on the video monitor.

"Mama. Mama. Mama."

Daisy is standing in her crib, calling for her mama and slapping her hands rhythmically on the crib railing. Looking at my phone, I see that it's only eleven thirty. Shay and I must have dozed off not long ago and dropped right into deep sleep.

I rouse myself and head toward Daisy's room. No sense in waking Shay up, too.

When she sees me, the kid starts jumping up and down, gripping the crib railing to steady herself. I've spent some time around her, so we're not complete strangers, but I'm clearly not the one she wants. She looks past me to the door and again calls for her mama.

"It's time to sleep, Daze," I tell her. "Back to bed for you."

"Daddy?" she says softly, still looking beyond me to the door.

The sound of her breathy voice makes me smile. She's a sweet kid, and I can clearly see why she's universally adored in the Rogue world. Whenever she's around the band, she's doted on and rarely touches foot to floor with so many people vying to hold her. But at just over a year old, she's getting big for that now.

"It's night-night," I tell her. "Time for sleep." When she doesn't automatically settle back into bed, I reach for her to ease her down. "Oh, you feel warm. Is that normal?"

"Mock?"

I have no idea what that means, and her temperature is starting to worry me. "Come on, you," I tell her, lifting her up out of her crib and holding her against my hip as I go back to the living room.

"Shay, wake up," I say. Shay doesn't budge, so I kick his foot. That only gets me a snuffling snore. I look at Daisy. "Can you believe this guy?"

"Mock." It's a demand from her now, but I still don't know what she wants.

This time when I go to kick Shay, I aim for his ankle.

"Fuck's sake," he yelps as he wakes. He reaches down to rub his ankle. "What's going on?"

"Daisy's up."

"What time is it?"

"Close to midnight."

"Put her back to bed, then." Shay leans back again and closes his eyes.

"Mock. Mock. Mock."

"She keeps saying that," I explain when Shay cracks an eye open to look at us. "What does she want?"

"Milk, you idiot."

"Oh."

I figure that's a good thing to help her cool down, and I take her to the kitchen. Placing her on the floor, I pour a cold cup of milk and then hand it to her.

"There you go, Daze. Have at it."

She contemplates the cup as if she's never seen milk in her life. Then she toddles over to the trash bin pull-out drawer and drops the cup into it.

"Bye bye!" she says with a wave.

"What was that for?" I ask her with a laugh.

"Mock?"

"You make no sense, kid. You know that? I just gave you your mock, didn't I?'

"Ba ba."

Now I get it. She just showed me what she thought of drinking out of a cup. It's still all about the bottle for her. I laugh, and she looks at me curiously.

"Bottle, got it."

After more trial and error, she lets me know in her own way that the milk needs to be warmed, then placed in a bottle, before she'll drink it. I sit her up on the counter, and we hang out together in the dim light while she drinks. I make conversation, but she has very little to say in return, most of her replies are giggles or stares. Once she's done with the bottle, I place it in the sink and hold her against my hip again. She still seems warm to me, so I return to Shay.

"Hey, wake up," I tell him. Before I can gear up for another precisely aimed kick, he opens his eyes. "Does she feel warm to you?"

That gives him pause. "Warm? Like sick?" He stands and touches Daisy's little forearm.

"Well, I don't think you can tell if she's got a fever by touching her arm," I say, suddenly feeling like I know what I'm doing with this babysitting thing.

"Right." He touches Daisy's forehead and cheek. "Yeah, she might be."

"That nanny said it was food poisoning. Do you get a fever from that?"

"I don't know."

"So, I guess we should take her temperature?"

Shay eyes me for a moment. "How do we do that with a kid this young?"

I shrug. My brief moment of confidence is gone. "Should we call Sophie?"

"Is it that big of a deal? Like interrupt their one night away, kind of big deal?"

"There's no way we would know. Couple of newbies at this."

"Yeah," Shay agrees. But it isn't an answer.

"How about you call Jessica. See if she knows what we should do?"

Shaking his head, Shay says, "She's great with older kids because of the school. But she knows as much about babies as we do."

"Great."

"How about Celia? We could check with her—"

"That would be pretty fucking awkward, right about now, don't you think? She and Marty are on the outs."

"Well, fuck, what do you suggest we do?"

This is just the nudge I didn't realize I was hoping for. "I've got an idea," I say.

45

When Ms. Patterson arrives, she looks like a fantasy come to life from my childhood fascination with Jennifer Beals of *Flashdance* fame. Ms. Patterson had obviously dressed hastily in body hugging jeans and an inside-out, off the shoulder gray sweatshirt. Her dark hair is down in loose curls and I've never seen her look lovelier.

"Shay, meet Ms. Patterson," I say when I've led her to the living room.

Shay had been entertaining Daisy by building block towers on the floor with her and now he stands to greet us.

"You can call me Amelia," she says.

"Amelia," both Shay and I say.

Hearing her first name is a novelty. I knew it, of course, back when I first started seeing her. But she had been so insistent on the formality of me using her surname, that this feels like I've been let in on a treasured secret.

She and Shay shake hands.

"It's good to meet the woman who has done so much to help my brother," he says.

"Oh, well—" she starts but is interrupted when Shay speaks again.

"Even going above and beyond to come to our aid here."

"Daniel said young Daisy was suffering and he was at a loss," she says carefully. "I couldn't say no."

All three of us look at Daisy who now appears to be the picture of health.

"You said she was burning up?" Ms. Patterson asks pointedly.

"So it seemed, Amelia." I try on her name again and it feels odd. I might have exaggerated Daisy's symptoms on the phone to Ms. Patterson in order to get her here. I had called her cell direct, using the number I saved from our Tulum call. My worry about the kid was real, but it seemed the only way to get Ms. Patterson's help was to play it up.

Ms. Patterson gives me one of her dubious looks before crouching down before Daisy.

"Hi Daisy," she says. "I'm Amelia. What do you say we get your temperature taken?"

"Take bath?" Daisy asks.

Amelia smiles and takes Daisy's hand. "Maybe, if you're running a little too hot. How about you show me your room first?"

Shay and I watch as Daisy leads Amelia toward her room. I realize I've got an ear-to-ear grin on my face.

"What's going on with her, then?" Shay asks.

"What? She's a lifesaver, is all."

"Does this fit within the boundaries of the whole doctor-patient thing?"

"She's not a doctor. She's a therapist."

Shay sighs. "Whatever." He falls in a heap onto the chair and rubs the back of his head roughly, closing his eyes. "You said she was working with you on making better decisions, yeah?"

"Yeah, that's part of it."

Leveling his eyes on me now, he says, "Maybe she can help you decide not to fall in love with her."

My brother's ability to read people is particularly uncomfortable in this instance. I have no idea how to respond, so I tell him, "You worry too much, kid. You always have."

"If you say so, Danny Boy," he says resignedly. "If you say so."

When Ms. Patterson reappears ten minutes later, she reports that Daisy's temperature was normal. She gave her a diaper change and has placed her back in bed.

"She might just be off since her parents aren't here," she says.

"Yeah, I could see that," I say.

As if on cue, we hear Daisy calling for her mama again.

"Thanks very much for coming over—in the dead of night, no less —Amelia," Shay says. He stands and nods to the monitor. "I'll go sit with her for a bit. See if that helps."

Once he's disappeared toward Daisy's room, Ms. Patterson and I stand and stare at each other awkwardly.

"Well—"

"So—" I start at the same time.

We both stop short and smile.

"Have a drink with me, Ms. Patterson," I tell her. "It's the least I can offer you after your kindness of coming here to help a couple of clueless bachelors."

She hesitates, and I can see her mind at work. This episode has already crossed lines of what's proper between us. Should she put an end to it, or is there really no more harm that can come from staying a bit longer?

"Okay, sure," she says.

I feel my heart swell in silent response.

———

After rummaging through Gavin's kitchen like I own it, I find an unopened bottle of thirty-year-aged Paul Beau Cognac, along with a couple of appropriate glasses for tasting the expensive brandy. Ms. Patterson has alternated between looking out of the window at the inky sea and watching me, and now she sits up straighter in her spot at the breakfast nook when I join her.

"Sláinte," she tells me and gently knocks her glass with mine.

"Sláinte agad-sa," I reply. It's the equivalent to "good health to you."

"Your Irish is well remembered."

I laugh. "A very low bar, if we're calling a common toast reply an accomplishment."

She eyes me before enjoying a sip from her glass, closing her eyes briefly with the pleasure of it. Leave it to McManus to have the good stuff.

"Were you a good student?" she asks.

"I was, actually. Made high marks. Not that I ever did anything with it."

"What would you have studied if you'd stuck with it?"

I think about this and take a drink of the smoky, spicy brandy. I didn't have the kind of childhood that allowed the freedom of imagining what I'd make of my life. I was too concerned with getting me and Shay through the day to have fantasies of adulthood.

"I dunno."

"Maybe psychologist?" she suggests.

"What makes you say that?"

"You're good at understanding how people work."

"Am I?"

"You knew I'd come tonight. You knew pretty early on that Jules was no good. You called upon Gavin, and Conor, and Martin for advice and got what you needed at the time."

"One, I knew you'd come because you have a baby nephew you adore—"

"How do you know that?"

"Remember, when we were on the phone when I was in Tulum? You kept getting those notifications because your sister was sending through photos of his first haircut?"

Her eyes widen for a split second.

"Two, I knew Jules was up to no good because it was like looking in a mirror. And three, I don't know what you mean about those guys."

She's still flustered but regroups. "I, em, I meant that your meetings with them weren't accidental. You needed something specific from each one of them. You walked away from those visits having either reinforced your suspicions or learning something."

I think about that before shrugging. "Could be you're right. Or could be I've just had a lot of years' practice at conning people to get what I need."

She's visibly taken aback by this suggestion. It isn't what she wants to believe. She's had a soft spot for me since the beginning, assigning me virtues and good intentions that were often overly generous. I have no illusions over the ways in which I've manipulated and hurt others just to get by. But it almost breaks my heart to see her considering this side of me at the moment, especially because I don't believe I've been conning anyone. I started to let that go when I hooked up with Shay again before they went back on tour and did an even better job of it when Roscoe found me. That dog kept me from hunting down a fix that very day. And he's been the thing that makes me think twice every time I try to convince myself I can control just a little hit of smack. I think of him being alone in Shay's house now and yearn to go get him.

"I suppose that's honest," Ms. Patterson says, pulling me from my distracted thoughts.

She still looks troubled by my comment. I've made her think that I could've been conning *her* all this time. But that's not the case and I need her to know that.

"Listen," I say urgently, leaning across the table and looking her in the eye, "you and I met at the exact right time. It was when I was *ready* to be a different person. I've never conned you. Honest to god, I've been brutally, utterly honest and myself with you. That includes the good, the bad, and the ugly. What you've seen with me is truly how it is. I wasn't trying to suggest anything else."

There's a stubborn set to her face as she watches me warily.

"I only said that because I'm not one to accept a compliment or believe I've got any special skills. You know I'm still completely lacking in self-worth. That that's what all the negativity is in my head, telling me I'm nothing and will always be nothing."

She softens, her frame loosening. Maybe it's the brandy. Or maybe it's that she actually believes me.

"Still, Daniel?" she asks softly. "It's still that way for you?"

If I say yes, then she will think she hasn't made a difference with our sessions. But that's not true. She's made a world of difference. More than she can ever really know.

"No, not exactly. I don't know how to really describe what it's like, what it's been like all my life. But that overwhelming sense that I have no value, that's faded. It's not gone. I don't know that it will ever be gone. But it's now something I feel like I can get my arms around. If I can't exactly control it, I feel like I have a fighting chance now. And you're a big reason why. *You*, my dear Ms. Patterson, have made a huge difference in my life."

She smiles, and I see tears cloud her eyes before she can blink them away. She occupies herself with taking a sip of the brandy and looking out the window.

"This," she says, grasping for a change in direction, "is an amazing home."

"You," I return, "are an amazing woman."

"Daniel—"

"Amelia, please. Let me just say thank you. Thank you for coming tonight. And thank you for not just putting up with me these last few months, but for really helping me figure my shit out."

I risk reaching out to hold her hand. She gives me the supreme pleasure of allowing it, and even squeezing my hand in return, if only for a moment. But that is enough.

46

Once back from his fly-by-night trip to Italy, Gavin is completely focused on efforts in the studio. I tag along for the ride as the boys find their rhythm and it's a thrill. The interest I found in the technical side that first day stays with me and I continue to try to absorb as much of it as I can.

This routine of getting to the studio by eleven and leaving around two or three in the morning comes to a sickening halt when all the guys get a devastating text message.

———

When I see Ms. Patterson the following day at our regularly scheduled session, it's the first time since I called her to Gavin's house to help with Daisy. She had canceled a full week's worth of our appointments after that, claiming conflicts she couldn't avoid. I hadn't thought much of it, but now I understand what the reasoning was behind it because she's back to seeming distant with me.

She's trying to pull up that protective wall of professionalism that she lost when we had a drink together. I don't have time for this game, though, because I've got real shit to deal with and I get to it right away, telling her about Christian Hale committing suicide.

"Oh, I'm so sorry," she says. "Were you close?"

"No, but I knew him a little. I spent time with him when the band was on tour in New Zealand. And to think he just gave it all up on a whim is incredibly disturbing."

"Of course, it is. I'm sure, however, that there's more to it than a 'whim.'"

"There may well be, but seeing the fallout is a miserable experience. Gavin was absolutely devastated. Then we all had this dinner at Conor's where it was supposed to be this great news—he and Felicity got married *and* she's pregnant—but it was no celebration. No one could really give them their due because of this thing hanging over the whole lot of us."

"And how does that make you feel?"

I sigh and let my hands drop heavily on my thighs. The snapping sound rings out in the room and startles Roscoe. Though my frustration at this trite line she refuses to give up is obvious, she says nothing more. Being the stubborn arse that I am, I let the minutes tick by.

"Does it make you think of your own mortality?" she finally asks.

The fleeting sense of victory I felt when she was the one to speak first disappears as I think of her question.

"Maybe that's what it was," I say softly.

"What's 'it'?"

"Em, the thing I've felt since we heard the news. It's a huge sense of *dread*. It descended over me in a way I can't really explain."

"Is it worry that you're at risk in the sort of way Christian was? I mean to say, that his suicide was a shock, of course, and most people must have thought he had his depression under control. But then it . . . wasn't. Does that make you worry about your sobriety being at the same sort of sudden and unforeseen risk?"

This strikes right at the heart of what I had been feeling, though I hadn't been able to identify it. I hunch over and pet Roscoe, needing the soothing and repetitive action to offset the impact of what she's said.

"Did you realize," she continues, "you've been sober for a year? Your anniversary was yesterday."

Tears spring to my eyes and I can do nothing to blink them away. I had no conscious realization of the date, but now that she says it, I know it to be true. This is the longest I've gone without heroin since I started at age eighteen. I swipe at the tears that won't abate.

"It's okay, Daniel," she says soothingly.

"I didn't realize," I say and get too choked up to continue. My heart is thumping in my chest and I suddenly feel hot.

Standing, I pull my leather jacket off and toss it on the chair behind me.

"It's a remarkable achievement," she tells me.

Though I nod dumbly, I can't absorb this. Everything comes rushing at me at once—the past year in which I toured with my brother and made my own real money for the first time in my life; finding Roscoe and being able to rely on him as both a pal and something to motivate me to stay clean; meeting Jules and learning what a taste of loving and being loved is, even if it didn't ultimately work out that way; realizing that I have unofficially become a part of a band of brothers with being able to count Gavin, Conor, and Martin as my friends, and mostly this journey I've taken with Ms. Patterson where she has not just corrected the course of my life and decision-making, but showed me that *I* have the actual power to do that. And all of that was without heroin.

The distance I've come overwhelms me to the point where I fall to my knees and truly let the tears flow, crying silently at first, and then completely uncontrollably.

I'm a mess, but I have no will to stop it. I need to let it out, both as a release and as a sort of victory cry.

Roscoe nudges at me with his cold nose, concerned. With my eyes tightly shut, I drop my hand to his head and try to reassure him.

But still, the release is so cathartic that I can't stop.

Then I feel something else touch me. I open my eyes halfway and see Ms. Patterson is standing before me. She's touching my hair in the gentlest manner.

I don't think. I just act. Wrapping my arms around her waist, I hold her to me and press my face to her belly.

When she doesn't pull away or say a word, but rather simply keeps stroking my hair, I hold her even tighter. She's patient, as she always has been where I'm concerned, and lets me pull myself together in my own time.

47

"Shall we wrap up our session with a refreshing walk around the block?" Ms. Patterson asks.

We've pulled apart and I've mopped myself up with tissues. The idea of getting out of the office is exactly what I need to push past my intensely emotional outburst.

"Absolutely," I tell her. "Anything to escape these horrible green walls."

She laughs, and her smile is gorgeous.

The three of us step out onto the street and find patches of blue sky among the clouds. The October air is crisp, and a breeze makes Ms. Patterson hug her arms to her chest. I take her arm and wrap it through mine, so we suddenly look the part of a couple taking a pleasant stroll.

"Oh, Daniel," she protests mildly but doesn't pull away.

"Think of this kindness as my anniversary gift."

"The milestone is important," she says. "But it doesn't guarantee anything. You need to stay vigilant. Keep recognizing your impulses.

Don't brush aside those voices telling you to give in to your old coping mechanisms."

"Well, we'll just continue doing what we've been doing with our sessions, yeah?"

"That's actually what I wanted to talk about when you came in today, before you told me about Christian and we got into yesterday being your anniversary."

A sinking feeling overcomes me.

"I have the impression you're about to say goodbye," I say with a nervous laugh.

She stops walking and I do too, facing her with a wince in anticipation of what she might say.

"Daniel, you and I both know I've lost my objectivity. I can't properly treat you because I'm too invested in you on a personal level."

Though I instinctively know what she's saying is true, I panic at the thought of breaking off our relationship. "No, don't you see— that's what's made us the perfect match! I would never have been able to make this kind of progress with anyone else."

"I have no doubt you'll find another therapist to work with."

I look up and down the street, feeling helpless and strikingly lonely. Then I hit on an idea that could make this turn of events all worthwhile. "Then, this frees us to be friends, right?"

She shakes her head and the gesture breaks my heart.

Just as quickly, I realize her refusing to have any kind of relationship must mean all the times I thought we connected beyond the professional level was all in my head.

"So, you're saying I'm *still* fucking seeing things to suit myself? That you were always *only* interested in me as a *client*, as some fucked up sap you needed to manage?"

I smack the side of my head with my open palm in frustration.

As she had done before, she takes my hand and gently lowers it.

"Go back to what I said a moment ago, Daniel," she says calmly. "I told you I was *too* personally invested in you. I admitted to having crossed professional boundaries. That was *real*."

"So why can't—"

"Because this is my career and I need to right the course I've strayed from. I need the time to examine how I let this happen, so that I can make sure it never does again. That includes *not* furthering our relationship."

"Is there any chance—down the line—that we could—"

"I can't promise that."

"But, but . . . you're not saying absolutely not?"

She hesitates and finally gives me a noncommittal shrug.

"I'll take it," I say quickly. "I'll take the *possibility* that I'll see you again, my dear Ms. Patterson."

She smiles and then laughs. And then she takes my arm the same way I had her do earlier, but this time she holds me with her other hand as well.

We walk on.

48

The next few weeks see me falling back into my loner routine. Gavin and the lads traveled to Australia for Christian's funeral. After that, they lost all momentum for returning to the studio.

Roscoe and I do our walks, our bit of watching *Fair City*, and otherwise wasting the days away. I don't see Ms. Patterson and I don't seek out anyone to fill her place. How can anyone do such a thing, anyway? Of course, I think of her all the time. It becomes a daily ritual, imagining what it would be like to have her as part of my life. Not that that gets me anywhere, but it's better than accepting it will never happen.

And then something odd happens.

I get a call from Martin, asking me to come over. When I hesitate to accept the invitation--he's never reached out like this, after all-- he adds that I should bring Roscoe, too. Seems he's thinking of getting his boys a dog and wants to do a bit of a trial run with my Roscoe.

When we get to his house, it's nice to see he's done some deco-rating to make it more of a home. He's now got two sofas facing each other with a coffee table set on top of a rug between them. When I glance over to the kitchen, I see signs of life, including a filled fruit bowl on the countertop and drawings by his boys hanging on the refrigerator.

The lads aren't over yet, so it's just Marty and me for a time. Celia's due to drop them by soon, then we'll all go for a walk to let the boys take turns minding Roscoe. The poor fella will have to endure a leash, but it's for a good cause.

Martin greets Roscoe familiarly. They got on well when we were on tour, so I'm inclined to think him getting a pup would be good not just for the boys but for him. Especially after his latest tabloid scandal. He and his American actress friend found themselves the center of attention once more—this time focusing on a trip they took to Prague.

"How's things?" I ask as we settle onto opposite sofas in the living room.

Martin shrugs but says, "Can't complain."

"Of course, you can," I tell him.

He laughs. "Well, it's that I shouldn't complain."

"Trouble with your girl?"

"Ah, she never was mine. I only ever had her for brief, wonderful, moments."

"I should introduce you to a barman I know."

Martin looks perplexed. "Who's that?"

"He's got that same sort of love-sick thing you have."

Shaking his head, he goes on the defensive. "What about you? What's going on with Julia?"

My brief sense of superiority in defining his emotions has deserted me with this question. "Em, well, nothing. Honestly, I've got nothing with her."

"And what *did* you have?"

I hesitate but there's no use. I'm not someone who holds back, no matter how much I've improved myself, thanks to Ms. Patterson's efforts.

"For a brief, crazy, moment, we were intense together, and for a second I thought it was going to be something, but turned out she was just a mind-fuck.," I say.

"And it's all over?"

"Yeah, it's all over."

"Back to it being you and Roscoe."

I could take offense to this, if I were to think he was trying to look down on me, at how little I have in my life, but I don't think that's his intention. He's a good guy and not one to make digs like that.

Reaching down, I pat Roscoe and he gazes at me with those soulful eyes. "Yeah, me and my boy are doing all right."

"That's good to hear. I know it stresses Shay that he's not close by. But you seem to be holding it together."

The sentiment is a nice one, but the way he eyes how my leg bounces relentlessly and how I pick at my cuticles shows he's still got some doubt. I've come to accept that even the people I know well will always wonder if I'm about to slip into my old ways. It's a reflection neither on me nor on them. It's just the way it is.

"I'm doing my best, Marty. That's all I can say."

"That's what we're all after, aren't we? Just getting by and trying to be happy."

"About that. Last time I saw you here at your place, I came away thinking that's what you were—happy. Is that still the case? Even with your girl not giving you what you want?"

"You mean, do I have any regrets about leaving Celia?"

"Yeah, I suppose that's the question."

He looks away from me and after a moment I see what he does. Through the sheer curtains of the front room windows, his three boys are marching down the sidewalk, Celia following them.

"I don't, no," he says, still distracted. A smile turns the corners of his mouth up. "This is how it's supposed to be: us being parents but not together. This is what we needed. What *I* needed."

I nod. Within a few minutes, he's demonstrating this by greeting Celia warmly and making plans for them all to go ice skating. I know

Martin's intentions because of what he just told me, but the way Celia's eyes light up reveals she's not yet on the same page. This contradiction in their perception of things will just have to play out, I realize, deciding not to intrude on things just for a reaction, like I might have done in the past.

49

The other odd thing to happen is Conor ringing me to see if I'm still into the idea of getting a motorbike. He knows someone looking to get rid of theirs cheap. I jump at the offer, and we meet up several times at the Sandyford Industrial Estate so I can get comfortable on the thing—and for Mr. Perfect to give me his tips, but I'm okay with that. The guy knows what he's doing.

After one of these sessions, I suggest we go for a real ride.

"Where about?" Conor asks, eyeing the skies.

It's a cold November day, but the skies are clear for the time being. Even if it rains, we're good. Per Conor's recommendation, I got the same rain gear he has.

"It's not all that far. Follow my lead—for once," I say with a laugh.

Conor shakes his head and rolls his eyes, but he puts on his helmet and gets ready to go.

I take the same route I had the day after Jules showed up to argue we should be together because we were both fucked-up. It's a pleasure to ride side-by-side along N81 when we can, and for me to take the lead other times. The bike feels good, like a natural fit. I'm content to just enjoy the ride as we pass into Blessington and begin our tour around The Lake. About halfway around, I gesture to Conor that we should make a stop at one of the inlets.

"This is fantastic," Conor says, eyeing the pebble beach and the fellas fishing down the way.

"Stumbled upon it a while back," I tell him.

Conor pulls off his backpack and stretches. I squat and try to skip a rock across the water but don't get more than the first plop right in. Glancing back to see if Conor saw my pathetic effort, I find him retrieving a rag from his bag. He crouches down and starts wiping down his bike and I laugh.

"You're fucking kidding me," I say.

He looks up at me. "What?"

"We're not even done with this ride, you know? Why on earth would you be cleaning your bike now?"

"You do things your way, and I'll do things my way," he says dismissively.

Standing, I go to him and watch a minute as he brings the shine of the chrome muffler back from under a layer of water spots and dust. This is his control freak tendencies on clear display and what has always irritated me about him. I'm about to scoff and walk off, but then something dawns on me.

"I used to be like you," I say.

Conor gives me a dubious glance.

"Really. When I was a kid, though. All I wanted was control and to know what was coming next. Because our loser parents couldn't manage to provide anything for us. So, I had to be the one to figure it out. And the more things I could sort out meant the more control I could have and the better I felt because of it."

Now Conor stands and eyes me.

I laugh. "I know, hard to picture, right? Me? Danny fucking Boy, the one with control? Well, I had no fucking choice in the matter. I had to be the one to handle things. I was the only one capable of that."

"You took care of Shay," he says simply.

"I did what I could—"

"You took care of Shay. And thank God you did."

I'm speechless at that. Not only do I *not* deserve thanks for taking care of my brother, but I never would have thought Conor would be the one to say anything of the kind.

"Your brother," he continues, "is a good man. All of us would do anything for him. And you did everything you could, too."

"That's where you're wrong. I took off as soon as I could. I started to hate the ways I had to control things. It flipped somewhere along the way so that I connected control with that unbearable pressure I was under. I wanted to be rid of it. To get, not just freedom from the kind of control I felt tied to, but to have the exact opposite of control. I wanted complete fucking chaos."

"And a fine job you did of that," he says with a cocksure grin.

I want to smack the smile off his face. Everything is always so effortless for him. He's never had to struggle a day in his life. Instead of hitting him, though, I say, "Fuck off."

He's not at all ruffled by that.

"I'm just saying, you go all out with things" he tells me. "It's either you being the one responsible enough to raise your brother when you were just a kid yourself, or it's you completely getting lost in drugs."

"Yeah, yeah," I grumble and turn away.

"At least that's how it was. I don't know that I'd bet on this, but it does look like you've found some kind of balance lately. More than I've ever seen, that's for sure."

That stops me. I hate the way his approval makes me feel. Why should I care what he thinks?

He starts toward me, then pauses to clap me on the shoulder, giving me a squeeze for good measure. "Keep it up." Continuing on, he retrieves a pebble and throws it into the lake. It skips four times.

And then I realize why I care what he thinks. Because he's Mr. Fucking Perfect. And if someone who has everything so well sorted and knows how to navigate life the way he does, has some confidence in me, then I should take it. But, for as long as I can remember, taking any kind of pat on the back or acknowledgement has been a hard thing to do. I always treat it with suspicion. Ms. Patterson says that's because I had no support from my parents from the very start, that I don't trust good things, even ones as small as compliments, because they're foreign to me. But she also always told me I need to accept the good people are willing to give, so I try.

"Em," I say, "thanks for that. And, em, I'm sorry for taking your guitar that time, you know?" I wince, feeling awkward with this whole thing.

Conor seems to read me because he looks back at me and simply nods. "How about a beer before we head home?"

I smile. "I know just the place." Thinking of the look on the barman's face at Murphy's Pub when I bring him Conor Quinn, guitarist for Rogue, turns the smile into a laugh. That'll give him something to sing about.

50

The final piece to this new puzzle of odd happenings in my life is Sophie inviting me over for supper on a Sunday night. I assumed I'd be just one of many, but turned out I was the only guest to dine with the McManus family.

Daisy greets me like we're old pals, which is nice. I spend some time with her on the floor in the living room, letting her get to know Roscoe. Luckily, the old boy is tolerant of her pulling on his ears. Any kind of attention, even that with the tinge of abuse, is welcome to him. I know the feeling.

When we sit down for dinner, Daisy insists I sit next to her.

"You two really bonded that night we were in Italy," Sophie says with a smile.

She's glowing. Her belly is pronounced now, their second child developing quickly in this latter part of the pregnancy. But she carries it well. I get the sense this type of scene, a quiet dinner at home with her husband and kid is exactly where she most wants to be.

"She taught me a thing or two that night," I say. "Didn't you, Daze? I know your language now."

Daisy smiles so big that it crinkles her nose. "Doggy!"

We all look around for Roscoe and find that he's leaning against the chair she's perched on with the aid of a booster seat.

"Traitor," I tell him and rub him about the ears.

"So, I think we'll plan on getting into the studio sometime in January," Gavin says. "You still interested in being around?"

He's positioned that question to be read two ways. I meet his eyes for a long moment and understand completely what he's asking. Will I be around *at all*? Or will I disappear like I've done so many times before.

"Definitely," I say, still meeting his eyes. "I want to be here. I want to be in studio with you guys, too. If it's cool with you."

Gavin nods and I know I've satisfied his intent in asking the question to begin with. It was his way of trying to protect Shay. He was the one to fill my shoes when I skipped out on Shay. The one to make sure Shay got through the rest of his growing-up years.

Sophie's prepared an obscenely healthy meal of grilled chicken breasts, roasted asparagus, and fingerling potatoes. Everything is seasoned so well, though, that I don't mind. Besides, I saw her prepping some sort of chocolate goodie for dessert.

"Conor tells me you two are thick as thieves with motorbiking," Gavin says and takes a drink from his glass of red wine.

Sophie cringes. "Oh, I wish you guys wouldn't ride motorcycles. It's so dangerous."

"Believe me, Conor has given me enough lectures about safety precautions that it's actually sunk in," I say with a laugh.

"I hope so. We want everyone to be safe," she says. She and Gavin share a lingering look. It's similar to the one I witnessed when I came around before, but not quite the same. There's something about it this time that expresses worry rather than just love and intimacy. It still shows their connection, though.

I wonder about all they've been through, with managing to overcome Gavin's bad behavior and Sophie's straying.

"What do you suppose it is that kept making you give each other a chance?" I ask. I don't think I'll ever be able to control my gob.

They both laugh and glance at each other again.

"Maybe you should take that one, baby?" Sophie says and busies herself with cutting a piece of chicken to feed to Daisy.

"Eh, sure," he says with a smile. "I'll tell you what it is, it's this simple and complex thing called love."

"Cop out!" I declare, grinning.

"No, not really. I mean it. Love is beautiful and powerful, but it has to be given oxygen to breathe. It has to be given a chance in order to really work its magic. Sophie and I kept giving each other a chance because we had to give the love we have a real chance."

"I know!" I say with mock excitement. "I bet you could write a whole song about that very thing."

"Don't ask a serious question if you don't want a serious answer, DB," he says.

I laugh. He's right. I shouldn't dismiss his explanation so quickly, but it made me think of Ms. Patterson and how we never had a chance, even though I *know* there could have been something good with us. Maybe even something called love.

Instead of addressing that, I pivot and say, "Aye, mightn't you try calling me Daniel?"

Gavin laughs. "I wouldn't know who you are as *Daniel*."

He said it reflexively, but it stings. I know Gavin and the other lads, Shay included, can't help but think of all I've done wrong and who I used to be. But, at least to me, it does feel like I've moved on—for the better.

"Oh, I don't know," Sophie says. "I think Daniel suits him. Sounds distinguished. Like he's seen a thing or two and . . . learned some along the way."

Jesus, I love her.

After a second, Gavin smiles. "I'll gladly call you Daniel," he says. "Christ knows we're all entitled to our second acts."

"Cheers to that." I raise my glass and Gavin and Sophie do the same. Daisy joins in with her sippy cup and we all laugh.

Dinner moves along without any more heavy talk, just easy banter. Daisy and I get on like a house on fire, and I offer to babysit if

Sophie and Gavin want to go out. They say they'll keep me as their backup in case the nanny gets sick again.

———

Over the next few weeks, I see both Conor and Martin again, and am repeatedly invited to Gavin and Sophie's for Sunday dinner. All this means my quiet days have become occupied with being a part of these guys' lives and it feels good. Not complete, but good.

51

By the time New Year's Eve is upon us, I've mostly pushed Ms. Patterson out of my mind. I go on my own to Sophie's annual party at her house since Shay's still in San Francisco. He'll be coming back soon so he and the guys can work on the next Rogue album. In the meantime, I enjoy the party and the good craic with the guys. There's top-tier champagne flowing, delicious food, and non-stop good-natured conversations all around. Sophie and Felicity are near to bursting in their pregnancies. It's a relief that some joy has returned to this group of people after Christian's passing.

Martin shows up late in the evening and Sophie's plan goes perfectly. She had invited his girl, the American actress Lainey Keeler, to be here to surprise him. Seems their reunion works like a dream because they end up making a show of it with passionate kissing right out in the open.

Their happiness triggers missing Ms. Patterson all over again and I steal away into Daisy's room. She's asleep, having worn herself out being the hit of the party earlier. The girl is a charmer, that's for sure.

Being as quiet as I can, I straddle the rocking horse in the corner of the room. My knees rest on the floor as I find Ms. Patterson in the contacts on my phone. I hesitate only for a second before calling her.

The ringing goes unanswered. She's either out celebrating the holiday and didn't hear the call, or she saw it and ignored it. I choose to believe she saw it and debated answering it so long that it clicked over just as she was about to take my call.

"My dear Ms. Patterson," I purr.

I might be a little drunk.

"I have done very well, I think you'll agree, in letting this much time pass before ringing you."

I'm not sure exactly what my aim was in finally reaching out to her.

"It's just that I miss you."

Ah, I said that part out loud, didn't I? Oh well, there it is.

"I do, it's true," I continue. "I miss seeing you twice a week. I miss your smile and your humor. And the way you humor me. I miss those lovely legs and wondering what color skirt you'll wear on the day."

I sigh.

"I'm sure you'll take me calling and saying all this as confirmation that the decision you made to cut all ties was the right one. I know you needed to do that for your own sake. I understand. But, I do miss you. I want to tell you what's been going on with me. And I want to know what's going on with you. How's your cat, Dante? And what about Max, your nephew? Have you recovered your equilibrium in your work now that I've gone?"

Pausing at that painful reality, I look up and see that Daisy is awake. She's lying on her back and watching me. To keep her from causing a fuss, I go to her crib and sit on the floor next to it. She pokes her hand through the railing and I hold her little fingers.

"Daisy's woken up," I murmur into the phone. "Yeah, I'm here at Gavin's for the holiday. Sophie holds a party every year, apparently. Makes everyone dress up. You should see me in this monkey suit I got on. Look pretty good, actually," I tell her with a laugh. "Anyway, I came in here to call you. Probably should have found some other room. The house is big enough. You'd ask me why I chose this one. Well, I'm looking at the answer. This little girl is a spot of sunshine. I don't know. Just something about her makes me happy."

I take a deep breath. "And I have been happy. Relatively, anyway. I've been doing good post-anniversary of the one-year sobriety thing. You were right. I've got these friendships now and it's . . . something good. It's just that there's something missing without you in my life. And not because I need you as a therapist. I just need *you*."

I laugh at my declaration. What a way to try to woo a woman. Drunk, with an endless voicemail.

"I do understand that I'm not doing myself any favors with this call. But it's almost the new year and you're on my mind, so I just couldn't stop from ringing you. So, there it is. I'll wish you well and hope you don't change your number after this. Maybe . . . maybe I could phone you again, just to leave a rambling message if nothing else?" I ask with a laugh. "Anyway, happy New Year, my dear Ms. Patterson."

Ending the call, I close my eyes and savor the thought that I might have said something to reach her. Then again, I might have just as easily ruined any chance I have of ever seeing her again. Daisy squeezes my fingers and I look at her.

"Well, Daze," I say to my little friend, "the damage is done either way with that call, yeah?"

She blinks at me before closing her eyes for good, drifting back to sleep. I'm nearly with her when my phone buzzes.

It's a text from Ms. Patterson.

I'm pleased that it's a simple emoji and not a notice to cease and desist. The graphic is a little party hat in honor of the New Year. That's all I need to keep believing our connection continues.

52

I t's all babies and studio time over the next few months as both
Sophie and Felicity welcome their little ones, and Rogue works
in earnest on the new album.

I won't claim to have mastered any special skills by sitting in with
the sound engineers, but I have learned a lot. On the rare occasion
when my suggestion for an adjustment is taken *and* accepted, I'm
over the moon. The entire crew is hugely tolerant of me and my new
obsession with this stuff, and I start to have aspirations of a full-time
gig with the band: lighting while on tour and sound engineering for
recordings.

After a steady routine of months in the studio, the final day
comes and the thought of closing up shop is hard to take. Shay must
read that in my face, because he takes a minute to pull me aside in
the back alleyway.

"This has been a fantastic experience, having you here day-in and
day-out," he tells me.

"Yeah, it's been good. Thanks for letting me tag along," I reply
with a laugh.

"You're part of this thing now, Danny Boy."

Even though I've successfully gotten Gavin and Sophie to call me
Daniel, no one else does. It's fine, especially with Shay. That's who I

am for him. Calling me Daniel would be just as odd as me calling him Seamus. You can't change your childhood impression of someone, which is why we can't change our names. By the same token, neither can we change the loyalty we've always felt for each other. It's in our blood.

"Well, that's all thanks to you." I glance away, toward the end of the alleyway where there is a barricade setup to stop the groupies from helping themselves to the back entrance of the studio. These guys still get starry-eyed girls—and some guys—shadowing their every move. The strangeness of it has worn away, but I don't think I'll ever get used it like they have. It's just a part of their lives now, the fact that millions of people want to follow their every move.

"Listen, you know I'm headed back to San Francisco tomorrow. I want you and Roscoe to come stay with us for a while."

I've seen Jessica a dozen times or more since that incident where I scared her to death, and she's outwardly accepting of me, but I still hesitate. I still feel like I'm a weight that would drag Shay down from the good thing he found with his girl.

"Come on," Shay says. "It'll be a couple of months during the summertime in one of the most beautiful cities on earth. We'll do some sailing and figure out the rest."

"I don't want to interfere—"

"I got this pre-approved, okay?" he says with a smile. "Jessica is good with you being there. I think it would actually be an opportunity for you two to get to know each other a bit better. 'Cause, let's face it, neither of you is going anywhere."

I laugh and my smile lingers. "You're really sure?"

"*Yes*, ya thick bastard. Now, come on—the wrap party awaits."

Sophie has arranged a dinner party for all of those involved in the recording of the album, including me. I'm looking forward to relaxing with this crew. *My* crew, I guess I should say.

I nod. "Onward, then."

———

I've kept up semi-regular phone calls to Ms. Patterson during the past few months. I give her updates on these new friendships I have with the lads and how the studio time is going. I ask her questions about her life that I know she won't answer. Because she never answers, not even with an emoji. I don't mind that she's kept up this distance. I understand that she's not able to respond for her own reasons. I content myself with this being a one-sided thing that I'm carrying on.

That is, until it comes time for me to make the trip to the States. Now, I want desperately to hear her voice. We may not actually be in real contact, but just knowing she was in the same city as me was of some comfort. Soon, I'll be thousands of miles away and I can't bear the thought that we won't be able to talk about it.

But just like all the other times I've phoned, she doesn't answer.

"My dear Ms. Patterson," I tell her. "I'd love for this call to be a proper conversation. I miss those with you. Anyway, I have news. Roscoe and I are going to San Francisco for a few months. Finally taking Shay up on his offer of having us out that way. So, anyway, I'm thinking I'll put an end to these calls. It's getting a bit pathetic, isn't it? Me blathering on in a recording to you." I take a deep breath. "You know what I'd love, though? I'd love for you to make your own visit to San Francisco. Make a trip out and we can be tourists together. Wouldn't that be something? I hear they're big on Irish coffee there. I could take you for a real drink."

I know that this is just fantasy, but it is a sweet one that I don't mind getting lost in.

"I'll text you Shay's address there, so you can come by anytime, yeah?" I say with a laugh. "Be well, Ms. Patterson."

53

There are acres of green grass called Crissy Field right on the San Francisco Bay near Shay's house and Roscoe adores them. We've been in the city for almost a month now. Sometimes Shay joins us in our morning walks and explorations all over the city. During those times, we vary between relative silence, talking about nothing important, and deeper conversations about our parents and childhood.

Shay's been much more successful in letting go his resentment over those things than I have. As we walk along the cliffs at Fort Funston, a new spot we're checking out for Roscoe's sake, he tells me how he was able to make peace with the shitty lot in life he had as a kid.

"Listen, I just figure I made it through, you know? I survived and there's no use in giving it more importance than it deserves."

This is typical Shay. He's always had this passivity with things. No matter how I might want to see him express his anger, that's just not who he is. I can see, however, in this instance, why it works. It's one of those tenants I learned in NA, about accepting the things I cannot control.

There are a half a dozen brightly colored hang-gliders perched on the edge of the cliff and I watch them for a moment. Roscoe has run ahead and though I can't see him, I trust that we'll find each other. We always do.

"I suppose," I finally say with reluctance. "But I still don't know how you can go visit those so-called parents of ours."

"To be honest, part of the reason I check in on them—other than to be sure they're managing to take care of themselves—is to remind myself of how far I've come."

"Why would you need a reminder? You're the best drummer in the world!"

Shay laughs and shakes his head, humble as ever. He'd never dare say such a thing about himself, but I believe it and have no problem shouting it from the rooftops. Or the cliff tops, as the case may be. Rays of sunshine are darting through the remainder of the morning fog, promising a lovely day. We're headed to the steep makeshift stairs that lead down to the ocean. My bet is that Roscoe is already down there making friends with sand crabs.

"The thing that has always stayed with me from our childhood," Shay confesses, "is the worry that I'd somehow end up like them. That I'd develop that disconnect they have. But Jess, she put an end to that for me. I know I'm not like them."

"*Of course*, you're not. I may have ended up a fuck-up drug addict, but even so, I've *never* believed for a second that I'd turn out to be as useless as them. Never thought that about you either, kid. Jesus, I'm sorry you did."

Shay shrugs and smiles placidly. "It's over and gone now."

"Good. Don't ever doubt yourself again."

"Thanks, Danny Boy."

I wave that off.

"I mean it. Thank you for all that you did for me. You sacrificed yourself for me. I can never repay that."

I look away, unable to accept this. Shay is the most generous person I've ever known. He's giving with his time and his money and his heart. I don't know how he managed to come out so well, but I'm grateful he did.

"Ah, it's not true," I say. "I should have done better by you, you know? I should never have tried to pull you into my shit. I shouldn't have run away."

"I get why you needed that. I don't—"

"There's no excusing it. That's the thing, Shay. That's what I've realized with Ms. Patterson's help. Justifying all my bullshit has to end. I can regret it, though. And I do. But I also have to be accountable for it."

"Then, accept my thanks, man," Shay says with a laugh.

Glancing at him, I say, "It's fine. It's how it was, like you said."

With a nod, Shay lets it drop, reading my desire to move on. I can't truly accept his thanks because it strikes too deeply in my memories. It brings back the abject fear I lived with when I felt solely responsible for raising him. He's right that, in the end, we survived. There's no real use in going backwards.

"Your Ms. Patterson sure was a lot of help, yeah?" he asks.

I smile, glad for the change of topic, even if it does bring back that longing I've felt for her. It's been over six months since I've seen her, and I was good on my word about not leaving her any more messages since that last one when I told her I was coming to stay with my brother. It's been bittersweet, but I have tried to let go my fantasy that she'd join me here.

"She was," I agree.

"Any chance you'll go back to seeing her as your therapist?"

"Nah. Our thing is over."

"You did fall in love, didn't you?"

I glance at him and then out in the distance where Roscoe is sniffing around near some driftwood on the beach. We've descended most of the way down the sandy steps and we're not the only ones. This seems to be a popular spot to bring your dog, which is a good thing.

"I suppose I can't deny that," I say. "Though, I'm only guessing since it would have been a first for me. Not sure exactly what it feels like."

"You know when it happens, Danny Boy," Shay says sagely. "You know."

If that's the case, then I did fall in love with her. I've had no other comparable feeling, yet I sense that I held something sweet and real for her in my heart.

Finally, down on the beach, I take a deep breath and look up toward where we started. The cliffs seem dauntingly high, and even more so when one of the hang gliders pushes off the edge and floats above us. I flash back to Tulum, to watching the wind surfers in the wild, white-capped water and my longing to jump into the fray, no matter what harm might come my way. That desire to unleash chaos feels like a long time ago. The realization that I don't have the same interest in that kind of self-destruction anymore makes me smile. That change has been a long time coming. I give a lot of credit for it to Ms. Patterson. But I also acknowledge the work that I've done to get here. It all comes back to the choices I make, after all.

"And so? What's it coming to with you and Jessica?" I ask, ready to shift the focus away from myself. "Marriage and kids, yeah?"

Roscoe comes bounding at us with a tennis ball in his mouth. It's not ours. He must have found it when he was nosing around. When he drops it at my feet it's covered in slobber. I pick it up and throw it as far afield as I can. Looking back at Shay, I find he's got a dopey grin on his gob.

"Marriage will come sooner or later," he says. "And it looks like we'll definitely be doing the kid part," he says.

I'm elated by the news that my brother—the best man I know— will be a father. I slap him on the back before hugging him tightly. "Congratulations, kid."

"Thanks, man." He can't keep the smile from his face, even when he says, "You wiped that dog drool all over my back, didn't you?"

I laugh in acknowledgement. He shakes his head and we keep walking.

———

When we get home at mid-day, I'm first up the stairs. I hear two women's voices for a second before they stop abruptly. The first thing I see as I get closer to the second, main level of the house, is a pair of lovely legs partially exposed under a red pencil skirt while sitting on a stool at the kitchen island.

Then I see her. She's paired the skirt with a casual white cotton top and several delicate, layered gold necklaces. Her hair is down and longer than when I saw her last. More than anything, she looks radiant, with cheeks flushed and eyes bright at the excitement and uncertainty of the moment.

I feel no such conflict in seeing her, only pure and overwhelming joy. She has taken me up on my invitation to visit me here, but we both know it's so much more than a visit. This is the start of something, and I'll do everything I can to make it work.

"My dear Ms. Patterson," I say, the smile so big on my face that it brings me close to tears.

"Daniel," she replies. She smiles and stands to receive me as I rush to her.

———

The End . . .
   Continue for a Bonus Excerpt

———

BONUS EXCERPT

Early in Looking For Trouble, *Danny Boy hears a brief story about Jules from Gavin. That was based on a section I had to delete from* Tangled Up In You. *I've included that section here so you can get more of the juicy details of what happened:*

Gavin had been sleeping for ten hours straight when the vibrating of his cell phone made it jump so much that it finally fell off the side table and clatter onto the floor, waking him with a start. When he opened his eyes, he was surprised to see that it was getting dark outside. The clock told him it was almost eight-thirty and it took him a moment to understand that it was evening. A quick glance at the empty side of the bed next to him told him Sophie hadn't come home like he had expected.

They had planned to meet back in Dublin after being separated by work—her for modeling gigs all over Europe, and him for touring in America. Rogue had the next ten days off before they would go to Latin America for a series of festival dates.

The band returned home the previous night and while Martin went straight to see Celia and Donal, Gavin, Conor, and Shay chose to have a drink together out on the town. The night had run long as they entertained conversation with the pub regulars and more and more of their hometown friends showed up to celebrate with them. When Gavin finally crawled into bed at eight in the morning, he fell asleep content with the knowledge that Sophie would be home, too, that afternoon.

Fumbling for his cell, which now had a cracked screen, he put an end to the buzzing with a swipe over Sophie's photo. She must have had a flight delay, he thought, as he collapsed back against a down pillow.

"Baby, it's me," Sophie said.

"Darlin', I know it's you, but, where are you?" He rubbed his eyes and cleared his aching throat, desperate for his self-prescribed medicine of hot tea with a shot of whiskey.

"I'm at Heathrow airport. I've got some bad news."

Gavin sat up, suddenly alarmed. "What is it?"

"I'm not coming home yet. I'll be there in a week."

"What are you talking about? You're an hour away."

"I'm at the airport because I have to go to a job in the Maldives," she said and he could hear the hesitancy in her voice.

Now he was sure he was still sleeping and this was a bad dream. "The what? You're fucking joking, right?"

"No, and I'm so sorry, Gavin. I miss you so much."

"Then you'd be here if that was true. What are you doing? We've had this planned. Fuck's sake, we haven't been together for going on *six* weeks."

"I know—"

"And what about our deal? The one we made that said we wouldn't be apart longer than three weeks? You promised to be the one to make that happen since I can't do much to change my schedule."

"I know I did. It's just, Henri hasn't been letting me turn down anything. He says I can't ruin the momentum I have now or I might never get these chances again."

Gavin closed his eyes and shook his head. "So, this is your priority, then? That's what you're telling me."

"I am coming home, baby. And then I'll be with you for the festivals. This is just a little delay."

"What about the principle of our agreement?" That wasn't really his primary concern, but he wasn't above using it to express his frustration with the situation.

"I'm still going to work on the three-week rule. But I got a last-minute invitation to go to this SI shoot and I couldn't say no. It could be such a big deal for my—"

"What? Your *career*? Please, Sophie. I thought we had some perspective here."

"Don't belittle what I do. Just because you don't understand it—"

"What's to fucking understand? You're happier to get your photograph taken than to be with me. You're the one making the choices here."

"That's not fair," she said, and he could hear the tears in her voice. "My plane's about to take off. I have to go."

"Fine. Go."

"Gavin, I love you."

"Then come home," he said stubbornly.

"I will. Just give me one more week."

"I may not be here when you get back."

"Wait a minute, what does that mean?" she asked quickly.

"Just that if you're going to do your own thing, maybe I will too."

"Baby, please," she whispered.

"Please, what?" he asked coldly.

"Don't do this."

Gavin closed his eyes tightly and tried to control his emotions. He understood that they threatened to overwhelm his better judgment.

"Darlin', be safe and call me when you get there," he finally said.

"I will. I love you so much."

"I love you, Sophie," he said resignedly.

———

Over the next few days, Gavin tried and failed to shake off his sullen attitude about Sophie choosing work over him. Now more than ever, she was what he needed to soothe his frayed edges. He'd been feeling an unexplained sense of foreboding lately, like something terrible was going to happen. Episodes like this had occurred before in his life, but he was usually able to shake that free-form anxiety. This time, it didn't seem like there was anything he could do to be rid of it. He missed having his wife by his side. He missed the easy way she knew how to manage him, to bring him down from the edge. He also missed her body. It had been forty-five very long days without her touch while he turned away scores of women eager to fill her place.

When Jules showed up at the house unexpectedly he didn't immediately register that she was one of those women. He was just happy to see a friend who would take his mind off of his worries.

"You all right?" she asked as he led her inside the house.

"Yeah, sure."

"You seem . . . off."

"You can read me, can't you," he said with a smile. "No, I'm okay. Could use a laugh, though. Glad you're here."

"Took a chance by coming by." Jules looked around the empty living room. "Sophie here?"

"Ah, no. She'll be back day after next."

"Working, then?" Jules asked with a smirk.

Gavin didn't want to get into it with Jules. It was clear enough she knew he didn't care for Sophie's modeling career, but he wouldn't bash his wife with his ex.

"Drink?" he asked.

————

One drink turned into many as they took turns playing DJ for each other, chatting idly, and smoking the weed she had brought.

Gavin had relaxed and was happy to have released that anxiety he'd been harboring. Then, Jules ratcheted it back up.

"What do you do with yourself when Sophie is away this long?" she asked.

They sat on the floor, leaning against the sofa, and he glanced at her without understanding where she was going with this.

"Whatever suits me, I suppose," he said with a laugh.

"She's . . . open that way?"

"Eh, well, you know, we're adults. We can manage ourselves."

Jules raised her eyebrows in surprise, but that response quickly changed to delight. She slid over so she was sitting closer to him.

"If that's the case, then I'd be happy to help you manage," she said. "You must be positively desperate."

The marijuana made everything funny and Gavin laughed again. "You're hitting on me, Jules?"

She wrapped her arm around his neck and toyed with his hair. "I'm open to it if you are."

"What? You're open to sleeping with me? How'd we get to that?"

"You said Sophie doesn't mind—"

"I said no such thing. Jesus, I don't need this from you, Jules. I thought we were good with being mates. Right?"

Pulling away from him, she blinked and shook her head. "I, em, I thought you meant you were free to, you know, play around. I mean, if it's just a physical thing, it can be totally harmless. I'm sure you're dying to get laid after all that time on the road."

"I am, it's true. But I'm also happy to wait for my wife for that. Come on, let's just pretend this whole thing didn't happen, yeah?"

He could see she was hurt and embarrassed. But she also wasn't ready to let it go.

"What she doesn't know won't hurt, though. And in the meantime, you'll get that release I know you need. Remember, I can *read* you."

The vision of their time together years ago, when they were just starting out in the music scene and everything was free-flowing, including their desire for each other, streaked through his mind. They did know how to have fun together, that's for sure. And it would be easy to reignite that, if only briefly. He also thought of the fight he'd had with Sophie over not coming home. If she knew that Jules was in their house right now, not to mention propositioning him like this, she'd be justifiably pissed off. She had never come to like Jules, not after how terribly things had gone at their first meeting. Still, for the briefest second, he liked the idea of, not sleeping with Jules, but Sophie being jealous over her presence. It would be petty retribution for her choosing work over him. But he quickly rejected that idea.

"Like I said, let's just pretend this didn't happen and move on," he said. "Get you another beer?" He got to his feet and started toward the kitchen before she could respond.

―――――

When he returned to the living room with fresh beers, Julia had shaken off the episode and they resumed their earlier, easy banter until they fell asleep in the early hours of the morning.

Gavin woke first and realized Julia hadn't really given up. He was sitting on the floor, leaning against the sofa. At some point, she had cuddled up next to him, her head on his chest and her hand resting on his morning erection.

That's what he told himself it was. He didn't remember any other stimulus to create this situation. But, knowing how relentless Julia could be, he couldn't really be sure.

Trying to carefully pull away from her made her reflexively grab him tighter. In response, he put his hand over hers to stop what was becoming not just awkward but painful.

Julia woke and assessed their situation quickly and to her own liking. She clearly read his move as wanting her to stroke him and so she did, adding sleepy kisses to his neck as she continued.

"Jules, stop," he told her.

"Why? When it feels so good. *You* feel so good," she said with a moan.

His body reacted despite what he really wanted. Why did dicks have to be so damn uncontrollable? The thing he could do was remove himself from this situation. He stood hurriedly.

"That was not at all what it seems," he said with a laugh.

Getting to her knees, Jules reached out to unbuckle his belt.

"Fuck's sake, I said no," Gavin told her, pushing her hands away from him.

"I'm confused." She looked up at him and waited for a response.

"I wasn't after this with you. I just woke up and we were like that, but it wasn't what I was trying to make happen, okay?"

She slowly got to her feet and rubbed her face. "If that's how you want to play it."

"Truly, I'm not playing any games with you. I meant it last night, about not even going there."

Wrinkling her brow, she played dumb and said, "What happened last night?"

And he was relieved that she was willing to let this go.

"Listen, I need a shower—"

"I could use one, too."

"You're welcome to the downstairs bath. And then maybe you should go? I need to do some prep for the next bit of tour stuff, and—"

"Got it." She smiled at him and shook her head resignedly.

"Thanks a million, Jules. You did take my mind off things last night. I appreciate that."

"No problem."

———

Gavin took his time in the shower upstairs. He needed to wash away the incident with Jules. It confused him because they had been doing the purely friend thing for years now. How had it so quickly gone back to her wanting him?

He was still pondering the question when he stepped out of the bedroom's en suite to find Sophie just arrived.

271

"Darlin'," he said, "you came back early." He was so happily surprised to see her that he didn't register how furious she was.

"Yes, sorry to ruin your plans," she said, her tone ice-cold.

"Plans?"

"I imagine you had something planned since I came home to find Julia O'Flaherty just out of the shower and cooking you breakfast in my kitchen."

"Fuck me," Gavin whispered.

"You got that right."

"No, no. She was supposed to have left, Sophie. This looks bad, but it's not what you think."

Sophie released an incredulous laugh. "I guess it was *my* mistake, then, right? I suppose me making the effort to come back a day early to surprise you was a terrible idea?"

"What? No, it's fantastic—"

"I mean, since you've already figured out how to replace me. Hope she's as good as you remembered."

He knew she had every right to be angry, but it still rubbed him the wrong way that she was jumping to these dramatic conclusions. She knew he had never cheated on her, that he only had eyes for her despite the many temptations he dealt with on a daily basis. But, here she was, eager to cast him as someone who would stray on a whim.

"Is that what you really think, Sophie?" he asked. "Do you you really think she's here because I just fucked her? Or can you slow down a second and let me give you the truth?"

As she looked up at him, tears rolled down her cheeks.

"There's really no reason to cry," he said. "You've got it all wrong, my darling wife. Nothing is happening with Julia or any other woman. She did stay the night—downstairs. And she did take a shower in the guest bath. That's it. We were up late talking, having a laugh. That's all."

"Thanks for being so . . . sensitive," she said. "I guess I was *stupid* to fear the worst when I came home to find your ex-girlfriend here— especially after the fight we had where you threatened to not even wait for me."

"I," he started and stopped. He struggled to come up with the right words to fix this.

His sudden lack of communication abilities was the thing to send Sophie moving toward the door, and it made him panic.

"Where are you going?" he asked, grabbing her hand.

She pulled away from him. "Just don't," she said softly.

He followed her out into the hallway and grabbed her from behind, wrapping his arms around her tightly. "Sophie, I'm sorry," he whispered into her ear urgently.

"Let me go," she said, prying at his hands.

"I can't do that."

In desperation, he lifted her in his arms and carried her back to the bedroom, releasing her on the bed.

"What are you doing?" she asked, letting her tears flow.

"I don't want you running out. I just can't have you leave like this," he said.

She threw up her hands in defeat. "Fine. I'm here. You tell her to leave, though, or I will."

"I'll be right back, then."

Gavin ran out of the room and down to the kitchen where he found signs of an egg breakfast being started, but did not find Julia. She had clearly, finally, realized she wasn't wanted there. Back up in the bedroom, he found Sophie at the window seat looking out at the backyard.

"She's gone," he said and was disturbed when Sophie kept her eyes away from him. "I swear to you, Sophie, though it may look bad, that's all it is—appearance. I know you know that in your heart."

"Were you trying to punish me for taking that work trip?" she asked.

"What? No, of course not. I didn't have a plan. I didn't even know you'd be back today."

Sophie glanced at him with watery eyes. "I wanted to make up with you. I wanted to surprise you."

Gavin went to her and kneeled by her side. "I'm glad you did, darlin'. Honestly. And I'm sorry about all this. About how I reacted. I was happy to see you and then you got the wrong idea and I just reacted badly. I'd never do anything to jeopardize us. You do know that, right?"

She took a shaky breath and watched him. It seemed she always had the ability to read him, to read what was in his heart. Sophie was the one who could do that, not Julia. Hell, Julia hadn't even been able to read whether he wanted to fuck her. If she couldn't understand that, how could she know anything else about him.

"I really hate that she was in my kitchen," she said with a pitiful laugh.

Gavin smiled as relief coursed through him. "I'll burn the whole thing down and we'll start from scratch, yeah?"

She nodded with a weak smile.

Pulling her into his arms, he held her tightly, vowing never to be so petty and stupid again.

———

End of Excerpt

———

ABOUT THE AUTHOR

Lara Ward Cosio is the author of the Rogue Series - books that feature complex, flawed, and ultimately redeemable rockers, and the women they love. When not writing, Lara can be found chasing her daughters around the house or at the beach, always with music on in the background.

If you enjoyed this novel, please share your thoughts in a review on Amazon or Goodreads

To learn more about the Rogue Series, visit: LaraWardCosio.com

You can also subscribe to a mailing list to hear about the next installment in the Rogue Series here: Sign Me Up

ALSO BY LARA WARD COSIO:

Tangled Up In You: A Rogue Series Novel

Playing At Love: A Rogue Series Novel

Hitting That Sweet Spot: A Rogue Series Novel

Finding Rhythm: A Rogue Series Novel

Full On Rogue: The Complete Books #1-4

.

Made in the USA
Las Vegas, NV
17 January 2022

41711744R00157